SHOCK
TO THE
SYSTEM

The Donald Strachey Mysteries
by Richard Stevenson:

Death Trick

On the Other Hand, Death

Ice Blues

Third Man Out

Shock to the System

Richard Stevenson

SHOCK
TO THE
SYSTEM

A Donald Strachey Mystery

St. Martin's Press ❧ New York

SHOCK TO THE SYSTEM. Copyright © 1995 by Richard Stevenson. All rights reserved. Printed in the United States of America. No part of this book may be used or reproduced in any manner whatsoever without written permission except in the case of brief quotations embodied in critical articles or reviews. For information, address St. Martin's Press, 175 Fifth Avenue, New York, N.Y. 10010.

Library of Congress Cataloging-in-Publication Data

Stevenson, Richard
    Shock to the system: a Donald Strachey mystery / by Richard Stevenson.
        p.   cm.
    ISBN 0-312-13610-2
    1. Strachey, Donald (Fictitious character)—Fiction.   2. Private investigators—New York (State)—Albany—Fiction.   3. Gay men—New York (State)—Albany—Fiction.   I. Title.
PS3569.T4567S74   1995
813'.54—dc20   95-34505
                                                              CIP

First Edition: December 1995

10   9   8   7   6   5   4   3   2   1

For Joe Wheaton

1

The voice was a combination of Locust Valley lock-
jaw and Marge Schott, by way of the Albany Gardening Club and
the Mary Lou Whitney Lounge at the airport Americana.

"I'm not gonna bullshit around," Phyllis Haig said, a little
louder than was necessary even amid the lunch-hour din at Le
Briquet. "Bullshitting around is not my style, you can ask anybody who knows me. I'm telling you, Don, I'm telling you
straight out, no bullshit, that I am convinced Larry Bierly killed
my son, Paul, for his money and then covered up the dastardly
deed by trying to make it look like suicide. Do you get what I'm
saying? Am I making myself clear? Larry Bierly is a murderer, and
the police are not doing beans about it, and I want to pay you
whatever your rate is—if it's in reason, of course—to put that
little pissant Larry Bierly in the caboose where he belongs." She
peered at me unsteadily across her uneaten arugula with Gorgon-
zola vinaigrette and corrected herself. "Calaboose."

Mrs. Haig seemed to have six or eight drinks lined up in front
of her and three or four cigarettes smoldering in each hand, but
there couldn't have been more than a couple of each. She was
well on her way to ruin—fifty-nine pushing ninety—but still
turned out with care and expense in pale blue—eyes, linen skirt,
jacket—and pale orange—hair, lipstick, tangelo sections among
the arugula.

When she'd phoned the day before, I'd suggested we meet at
my office on Central, but she didn't like the sound of the address
("Is it safe to park a car up there?") and proposed lunch instead

at Le Briquet. Situated on a shady lane off State Street down the hill from the Capitol, Le Briquet catered to the comfortably well-off general public but existed mainly to provide highly enriched nutrients and hydration to New York State's elected representatives and their paid staffs. These meals were customarily compliments of the pols' fellow diners, officers of business and professional associations with an interest in the legislature's proceedings. It was a place where your car was safe, if not your soul or your wallet.

I said, "I knew your son and Larry Bierly slightly, Mrs. Haig, if they were the couple I'm thinking of. Weren't they lovers?"

She sniffed. "If that's what you want to call it, 'lovers,' " she said dejectedly. "It's not easy for a mother, Don." She fired up another two or three more Camel Lights. "You know, Don, when my daughter, Paul's sister Deedee, went through the entire basketball team at Albany High before she was seventeen, I wasn't crazy about it, but I survived. I figured, What's a little fornication among the young? Am I right? This was before AIDS, naturally, and Condoms 101, so what the hoo. I knew Deborah would outgrow her throwing-it-around-for-nothing phase, and she did, years ago. But when Paul went through the boys' swim team, that was another matter. You can imagine your daughter with some guy's big, stupid hard-on jammed in her jaw, but not your son. Do you get what I mean? Am I right? Try to put yourself in my place."

I said, "Yours is not an uncommon reaction among parents, Mrs. Haig."

"Oh, I know what you're thinking. It's PC now to say it's all the same—women and men, women doing it with women, men and men acting like real couples and shoving it up each other's patooties. But it's not the same. I know it, and I think you know it, Don. It's not what nature intended. Yes, my son was a homosexual, and he was crazy enough to go off with that little fart Larry Bierly and flaunt it in Lew's and my face. Lew was ripshit, as you can imagine, but not all that surprised. Paul wasn't the first Haig, Lew always said, who might've been better off in the bughouse." She took a long drag and shot a smokeball across the room.

2

"But that's my point, get it? Sure," she went on, "Paul was a prime candidate for the bin. But that's just the way he was, another Haig who was a little off plumb, and he was used to it. I'd kid him about it and we'd laugh. Did Paul get depressed sometimes? You bet he did. But who doesn't, am I right? So you go out and have a couple of drinks and get on with your life. Paul and I put a few away together, so I should know. The last time we tied one on was right after Lew died. Anybody wants to get depressed, they can get depressed about that. Pancreatic cancer—don't ever pick that one up, Don."

Another drag and another blunderbuss shot. "But what I'm telling you, Don, is, that's *it*. When life unloaded on you, Paul coped. He'd get knocked down and he'd bounce right back up. Paul was a survivor, like his old ma. That was one thing we had in common. It was his style to get the hell on with it. I know that about Paul as well as I know anything on God's green earth, and I know Paul would *not* destroy himself. Paul did not—Paul never could—commit suicide. And if Paul didn't kill himself, then it stands to reason, if you ask me, that somebody else did. Am I right? And that somebody—I'll bet the bank on it—is that miserable little faggot Larry Bierly."

She sucked up another slug of her Dewar's and gave me a look that dared me to contradict a single word she'd spoken.

I said, "I catch the drift of what your suspicions are, Mrs. Haig, and why you might want to hire an investigator. But I'm a little unclear as to why you went out of your way to consider hiring a gay detective—this is known about me around Albany—when you have, to put the most generous interpretation on it, conflicted feelings about homosexuals. Can you clear that up for me, Mrs. Haig?"

"Call me Phyllis," she said.

"Phyllis."

"Well, Don, that's a reasonable question and it deserves an honest answer. Number one, this is business. Lew always said that in the business world you have to consort with people you wouldn't dream of letting past your front door. And in return you can usually expect those people to be nice to you even if the ground you walk on makes them want to heave. Take you, for instance. You've been listening to me badmouthing gays for the last five minutes, and all you've done is sit there picking the label off your beer bottle. You're not doing what you feel like doing, which is to get up and reach across the table and wring my neck. Because this is business. Am I right?"

"You nailed me on that one, Phyllis."

"You bet. I've got a fat checkbook in my handbag, and you haven't taken your X-ray vision off of it since the second I sat down."

"I always like to share a moral outlook with my clients," I said, "but it's not a requirement. Prompt payment can sometimes form a bond too. In your case, however, Phyllis, even beyond considerations of differing outlooks on life and the human personality, if I were to consider taking your case, I'd need to know more about the basis of your suspicions of Larry Bierly, and about how and why you think I might confirm your suspicions. Those are serious charges you've made against Bierly, Phyllis."

She raised one of her tumblers. "I like you, Don, you know that? You and I are on the same wavelength. Jay Tarbell knew what he was doing when he suggested I get in touch with you. Jay's the main reason I called you, of course. You come well recommended."

"I've never been personally associated with Attorney Tarbell. But I know him by reputation, and I know he knows mine."

She crushed her butt end in the overflowing ashtray and shot a final volley of smoke over my shoulder and into the next room. "Jay's just another lawyer. Let me tell you about Jay Tarbell. One time Lew ran into him out at the club and asked Jay what he knew about Randy Hogan, the boy Deedee was engaged to at the time. Jay knew next to nothing at all—just some stupid crap about the Hogans suing the dog groomer who snipped off their Lhasa apso's business by mistake. A week after their country-club encounter, Lew received in the mail a bill for one hundred and eighty-five dollars. That's lawyers for you. I'll probably have to

4

auction my grandmother's dentures to pay Jay for recommending you. So I hope you aren't going to let me down—or take advantage of me now that you know that I'm a helpless widow." She gave me a caricature of her idea of a helpless-widow look. It was hard not to glance around to make sure nobody I knew was witnessing this.

I said, "My fee is four hundred dollars a day, plus expenses. A retainer of twelve hundred dollars is customary. Unearned parts of the retainer are refundable. Sometimes I work cheap for the poor, and if you want me to have a look at your tax returns I might make an adjustment."

The helpless-widow look faded. "That's awfully stiff."

"You'll find it's average among private investigators you would consider hiring."

"Four hundred dollars used to buy people like you for a month."

"Not anymore."

"A hundred and fifty seems reasonable."

"Uh-huh."

She popped another cigarette out of a nearly empty pack on the table and used a butane torch to ignite it. The smoking section at Le Briquet was in a separate room from the nonsmokers and was about as freshly ventilated as a Russian airliner.

She said, "You know how to tighten the screws on an old widow."

"It's just business."

She looked for an instant as if she might spear me with a rejoinder, but then something in her slumped. She looked thoughtful for a long moment, before gathering herself and stating in a businesslike way: "The reason I want to hire you, Don—for your standard fee, even though it's goddamned highway robbery—is exactly what I told you on the phone yesterday. Paul's death on March seventeenth, two months ago yesterday, was ruled a suicide by the Albany Police Department and by the coroner. That's plain nuts. Paul got the blues once in a while, but he was never—*never*—so depressed that he would do away with

5

himself. That I can tell you with a hundred and fifty percent certainty. Anyhow, Paul and I did lunch at Shanghai Smorgasbord the week before he died, and everything was hunky-dory with him. Paul had been on Elavil for over a month when we had our lunch, and I can tell you without fear of contradiction that it had done wonders for him. He was more relaxed than I'd seen him in ages. He looked good and he sounded good. The only thing that seemed to be eating at him a little bit was, Larry's business was in trouble."

She gave me a significant look and at the same time sent her radar to a passing waiter, who spun in his tracks and asked if he might refresh her Dewar's and my Molson. I said I was ready for coffee; she just nodded.

"What kind of business is Larry in?" I asked. "Does he still have a mall gift shop?"

"That was Paul's," she said glumly. "Beautiful Thingies, out at Millpond. Larry's is out there too, Whisk 'n' Apron. But Larry borrowed heavily to buy his franchise, and his bank was threatening to call in his loan. Paul said Larry was six months behind with ConFed. Paul wasn't overly communicative when it came to Larry. He'd heard my feelings on that subject any number of times, and I suppose he didn't especially want to get World War III going. But I dug it out of him about Larry's financial problems, and it's just lucky I did. There's your motive, am I right?"

"It could be."

"The tragedy of it is, in spite of all the rocky times those two had—screaming and hair-pulling and moving in together and moving out again—Paul never took the time to have his will changed. And now Larry gets *everything*—Paul's stocks, bonds, cash. Even the business, and Beautiful Thingies is—it's a goddamned gold mine, is what it is."

"Are you contesting the will?"

This elicited an uninhibited raspberry. Three suits huddled at the next table glanced our way briefly, then resumed plundering the Treasury or mauling the Constitution. She said, "It's airtight, Jay says. Unless we can prove Paul was mentally incompetent when the will was signed, or he was forced. Being dumb as bricks isn't enough. Larry gets it all. That little tramp must have been great in bed, is all I can say."

I said, "Did your late husband leave you his estate?"

"Yes, he did. Not that it's any business of yours."

"Did he leave it to you because you were great in bed?"

"Yes," she said, missing not more than half a beat. "I'm sure that was a big part of it." The waiter deposited her Scotch in front of her. "Thanks." She sampled it and found it up to par. "I successfully feigned interest in making love to my husband right up to the day he was too sick to want to do it anymore. I also loved my husband and made a home for him and raised his children. That's called a marriage—and is recognized as such by the State of New York and is honored throughout the land. That marriage is the very good reason that I am the beneficiary of Lew Haig's estate. What else would you like to know about me, Don?"

"I guess I know all I need to know about you for now, Phyllis. You're quite a remarkable piece of work."

"You bet I am."

"Tell me more about Paul's death. The papers, as I recall, said he died from a drug overdose."

"Elavil and Scotch," she said, raising her glass by way of partial illustration. "At least a thousand milligrams of Elavil—that's over a week's worth—and a fifth of Paul's beverage of choice. They found Paul in his apartment on the morning of Friday, March eighteenth. When Paul didn't show up to open the shop, some of the help went over to Whisk 'n' Apron and Larry went to Paul's apartment and found him, he said. I'm sure he knew right where to look."

"They weren't living together at the time?"

"Larry'd had his own place since the first of the year. He told Paul he needed his space, Paul said. I'm sure he was sneaking around. Paul lived on Willet Street. Larry has an apartment elsewhere in Albany. I really couldn't tell you where. I was never invited."

"Would you like to have been?"

"Don't make me laugh."

"Was it the amount of Elavil that ruled out an accidental overdose?"

"That's what the police said, and I'll give them credit for two watts of brainpower on that one."

"Was there a suicide note?"

The waiter brought my coffee. Mrs. Haig's Joe Camel was nearly spent and she used it to light a new one. "Oh, there was a 'note,' all right." She waggled her fingers dramatically to indicate quotation marks, ashes and sparks flying. "It was exactly the type of 'note' you'd expect." She gave me a look of bright-eyed disgust.

"What type of note was that?"

"Not handwritten. The 'note' was on Paul's computer. It said, 'I love you, Larry. I'm sorry. Paul.' Any fool can see that Bierly put it there himself, the goddamn conniving little homicidal piece of shit."

"He could have," I said. "But what makes you so sure he did, Phyllis? What evidence have you got beyond Larry's financial problems and the fact that you don't happen to like him? This is awfully thin stuff you're presenting me with—a combination of resentful-mother-in-law-ism and vague circumstantiality. It's not much to start out with, and probably grossly unfair to Larry Bierly."

She gazed at me levelly and said, "That's what the police thought too. But there is something about Larry Bierly that you ought to know, Don. Just because it's not on the official record, the police pooh-poohed it. But I've got the lowdown on Mr. Larry Bierly. I got it from Paul. Larry Bierly is a violent man. He once assaulted a man and threatened to kill him. This was all recorded on tape, but the man didn't press charges because Paul bought him off."

She watched me with cool expectancy. I said, "Who was this man?"

"Vernon Crockwell."

"Vernon Crockwell, the psychologist?"

"That's the man."

I said, "Even if Bierly had carried out his threat and murdered Crockwell, a lot of people in Albany would have considered it justifiable homicide."

Phyllis Haig neither laughed nor exclaimed over this. She just opened her bag and confidently pulled out her checkbook.

2

Back on Central, I phoned Larry Bierly at Whisk 'n' Apron and set up an appointment, then reached Timothy Callahan at his office at the legislature.

"You knew Paul Haig, didn't you?"

"Slightly—why?"

"Did he strike you as depressed?"

"Well, he killed himself."

"Other than that. Just what you saw."

"More anxious than depressed, I'd say. But I hardly knew him, so I'm not the best person to come to for an insightful diagnosis of his mental state. Why do you ask?"

"I'm coming to that. It's problematical. Was Haig the guy we'd see sometimes with his boyfriend at gay political events—him a tall blond with wavy hair and the boyfriend darker and chunkier? And they were always a little shy and nervous and apart from everybody else?"

"That's them. Larry something was the boyfriend."

"Larry Bierly."

"I tried to get them more involved, or at least to feel more at ease. And they were perfectly nice, and friendly, but they never seemed able to mix and get to know people and really relax."

"You're ever the thoughtful host, Timothy, whether it's brunch for twenty-two or an assault on the Senate Republicans."

"Thank you."

"They both must have friends in Albany. Any idea who?"

"Yes, but it would be easier to answer these questions if I

10

understood the context in which they were being asked. What's this all about?"

After nineteen years, he still needed explanations from me. If being willing to speak at length into an unresponsive void isn't one of the cornerstones of a rich relationship and enduring love, what is?

I said, "I'll get to the point, trust me. Just tell me what you know about Haig's and Bierly's social life, if any. Don't think context. Pretend we're deconstructionists."

He let out a little sigh that was so recognizable I could almost smell the tuna he'd had for lunch. He said, "Both Bierly and Haig owned and managed businesses out at Millpond. But you already knew that, right? We've seen them out there."

"Right. Bierly runs Whisk 'n' Apron and Haig owned Beautiful Thingies."

"Well," he said, "I *have* seen Paul Haig somewhere else."

"Where?"

A little tuna-scented silence. "You're going to consider this somewhat pompous," he said.

"Uh-huh."

"I'm not sure of the ethics of my telling you where I saw Haig."

"Oh, the ethics."

"I'm afraid so."

Now Timmy was neither a psychiatrist nor an attorney. Nor was he a priest—although at fourteen he had briefly entertained the idea of becoming one, in which calling he would have been able to wage holy war on his newly discovered unholy sexuality while at the same time dressing and undressing with men. By fifteen, though, he had discovered both liberation theology and Skeeter McCaslin, with whom he enjoyed a sweaty, Clearasil-slick affair for over two years—until they both had graduated from high school and left Poughkeepsie—that was carried out with the stealth of Mossad's operation in getting Adolf Eichmann back to Israel. I once asked Timmy if "Skeeter" was short for "Mosquito"; he just laughed and said most assuredly not.

I said, "Let me guess why you have ethical doubts about telling

11

me where you saw Paul Haig. Does it have something to do with covert U.S. government activities for dealing with North Korea's nuclear-bomb program?"

He laughed lightly. "I knew you'd see my reaction as kind of—morally overweening."

"Your term, not mine."

"The thing is, if I told you why I'm reluctant to tell where I saw Haig, you'd understand my point. But then you'd also know where I saw him, and I'm the one who would have told you. Can't you just take my word for it that I shouldn't tell you where I saw him? Trust me. Like I'm trusting you."

I said, "Paul Haig's mother is convinced Larry Bierly killed Haig and made it look like suicide. Haig and Bierly were on the outs, she says. Bierly was the beneficiary of Haig's estate and needed money to save his business, according to Mrs. Haig. She told me Bierly has a history of violence and once assaulted and threatened to kill a man. Mrs. Haig wants to hire me to prove the coroner was wrong and the suicide was murder and have Bierly charged. The mother is something of a horror show herself, and I'm trying to evaluate whether or not to hire myself out to her. That's why I'm asking you these questions, Timothy. Now are you going to help me out?"

"AA," Timmy said.

"As in Alcoholics Anonymous?"

"That's where I've seen Haig—with the AA bunch that hangs out on the sidewalk in front of Saint Aggie's before their meetings."

"More than once? He was a regular at that meeting?"

"I'd say off and on over several years. When I worked late and walked home in warm weather, I'd sometimes pass there while they were out smoking and drinking coffee on the sidewalk before the eight o'clock meeting. Sometimes I'd say hello to Haig and he'd say hi back."

"What about Bierly? Was he ever there too?"

"Not that I ever saw. I just saw Paul Haig."

I said, "Timmy, I don't think it's unethical for you to pass this

12

on to me. AA members are morally bound to protect the privacy of other members. But you're not a member. Anyway, you're telling me, not *Le Monde*. So what's the big deal?"

"I'm not a member, but I respect AA's confidentiality ethic, and the best way I can show my respect for that ethic is by observing it."

"So by walking past their meeting you fall within AA's ethical penumbra?"

"Yes, I believe I do."

Now it was he who must have gotten a whiff of my gnocchi breath. I said, "Then I appreciate your ethical lapse on my behalf."

"You're welcome to it this one time. It's no big deal. Do you really think Bierly might have killed Haig? I thought Haig died of a drug overdose."

"It was a combination of Elavil and Scotch. The mother is something of a boozer herself and maybe delusionary. But the one thing that's more or less plausible in her account is that she knew her son's mental state and she's certain he had not been suicidal. So I'm going to ask around a little and talk to Bierly before I decide whether or not to take Mrs. Haig's money. She stuffed a retainer check in the bun basket at Le Briquet and shoved it across the table toward me, but I handed it back for now. I'm meeting Bierly for an early dinner at Millpond, so I won't be home until eight or nine."

"I'm glad you're meeting Bierly in the mall if he's violence-prone."

"That's Mrs. Haig's story, but who knows. It is her assertion that after Bierly attacked someone, the guy was going to press charges, but her son bought him off before the cops were notified. And here's the intriguing part. The man Bierly supposedly threatened to kill was Vernon Crockwell."

This elicited a sound that was part guffaw and part snort. "My, my. Herr Doktor Crockwell. Was Bierly in Crockwell's treatment group—getting cured of his sexual deviancy?"

"They both were. It's where they met, according to Mrs. Haig."

"If subjecting yourself to Crockwell isn't incitement to murder, I don't know what is. No wonder Bierly is full of rage and confusion. It sounds as if you should approach him very gingerly, Don."

"I'm meeting him in a mall pizzeria, not in a dark alley. But from what I know of the homosexuality cure programs, people tend to come out of them either zombielike or with a healthy anger directed not at themselves or one another but at the programs they were victimized by. So, not to worry."

"I will. I do."

"I know. Maybe I'll bring you a lovely gift from Beautiful Thingies to help you feel better. A Gucci waterpick cozy. Or a Georg Jensen nipple ring."

"Just watch out for your own beautiful thingie."

"I'll make a note."

3

The darling buds of May had popped out even on the genetically stunted arboreal species around the Millpond Mall parking lot, and the air was fresh after a spring shower. All but glacier-ridden from November to March—and hot and sopping as Bangladesh in summer—Albany during a brief spring and briefer fall was not only fit for human habitation but certifiably pleasant. Crossing the newly washed tarmac, I'd have felt downright jaunty if I'd driven out to Millpond for a movie or a pack of clean sweat socks instead of an interview with the object of a scurrilous accusation of homicide that was conceivably true.

Bierly had suggested we meet at the Irish-pub-style pizza-and-beer joint across from the cineplex (Timmy had once said, "The pizza here is definitely Irish"), and I spotted Bierly at a table in the back, away from the bar and the sports rowdies.

"So, what did Phyllis have to say about me?" he said, looking curious and mildly skeptical but with no apparent fear of what my answer might be. I had told him on the phone only that I was considering investigating Paul Haig's death for Mrs. Haig and that she had suggested I interview Bierly.

"Her opinion of you is poor," I said, pulling up a chair. "But I'll bet you already knew that."

He laughed, but without amusement. "When Paul and I lived together, she'd get lit and call the apartment about once a week. Whenever I answered the phone, she'd start off by saying, 'Well, if it isn't Buttfucker Bierly.' That says it all about what Phyllis Haig thought of me. It also tells you what she really thought of

15

Paul . . . although she'd never admit what she actually thought of Paul—even to herself. To her little boy, who could do no wrong, she was nice as pie."

He said this less with bitterness than with bemused resignation. What I had taken to be shyness when I'd seen Bierly at gay political events now seemed another kind of reticence altogether, the holding back of a man with reduced expectations of how other people were going to regard him. I remembered him more clearly now, and he hadn't changed since I'd last seen him: about thirty, with curly black hair and big, wary dark eyes in one of those pleasing but not-quite-locatable, all-over-the-map American faces that suggest some of each of the auld sod and the Rhine and Calabria and maybe even pre-Columbian Vera Cruz. He looked muscular under the white dress shirt he had on, sleeves rolled up to mid-forearm, with a paisley necktie roller-coastering down a well-developed chest.

I said, "Mrs. Haig believes that Paul did not commit suicide. She told me he was not depressively suicidal and would never have taken his own life. Did you know that this was her belief?"

A curt nod. "Oh, I certainly knew that."

"She told you?"

A hard look. "The police are the ones who told me. Phyllis and I have not spoken since Paul's funeral in March." He watched me grimly, waiting for what—it now dawned on me—he had known was coming since I had sat down.

Dragging it out unnecessarily, I said, "And the police raised the possibility with you that Paul's death might not have been suicide?"

He grunted. "They did raise that possibility."

A waiter in a white shirt and black bow tie appeared and asked if we were ready to order or if we needed a few more minutes. I asked for a draft and said we needed a few more minutes. After the waiter went away, I said to Bierly, "What evidence did the police have that pointed away from suicide toward accidental death? Or homicide, of course."

16

Bierly had been absently rotating a beer glass on the tabletop, but suddenly he stopped. "Now look. I know she thinks I killed Paul," he said tightly. "So let's just quit playing these fucking games. Can we just do that?" His face was red and the muscles in his forearms were taut, and he didn't look so philosophical anymore.

"That suits me," I said.

Bierly started rotating his glass again, faster this time. "One of the cops told me the line of crap she gave them—I was violent, and I was jealous, and I was a crazy queer who murdered Paul for his money, and I tried to cover it up by making it look as if her happy, well-adjusted little boy had committed suicide. Jesus, that woman!" Veins throbbed at the sides of his temples and on the big hairy hand that worked the beer glass.

I said, "You and Phyllis didn't hit it off too well, did you?"

This poor attempt to lighten Bierly's mood failed. He said, "She hired you to get me, didn't she?" Now the veins were bleeping faster. "The police checked me out and found out I had an alibi for the night Paul died—I drove my landlady to Utica, where her daughter had been in a car crash, and we didn't get back until four in the morning—but of course that wasn't enough for Phyllis. Phyllis knows what Phyllis knows. How much is she paying you to frame me, or just harass me, or whatever it is this is supposed to be?"

He regarded me as if I were a plague bacterium deserving of fear, scorn, and, if it could be arranged, extermination. I said, "I have no interest in persecuting you, Larry. I haven't agreed to actually work for Phyllis Haig. I wanted to talk to you first. That's why I'm here. I'm not sure I want to get mixed up in this at all. The situation would interest me only if I became convinced that Paul Haig had actually been murdered. But you seem to be telling me that that was not the case."

The rotating beer glass came to a halt. "Oh, is that what I seem to be telling you? I don't think so."

"You're *not* telling me that Paul wasn't murdered?"

17

The waiter came back with my draft and asked if we'd like to order or if we needed a little more time. I said we needed a little more time.

Bierly eyed me levelly and said with what looked like carefully controlled emotion, "Of course I didn't kill Paul. Phyllis is—she's a serious, out-of-control alcoholic, and her brain is—she's a crazy, obnoxious old booze hound. Even when she's sober she's a chronic liar. Probably all the Haigs are. Paul was. Based on what Paul told me about him, his father was a liar too. Unless Paul was lying about that."

He blinked away something he didn't seem to want to remember and went on. "But the fact is, I loved Paul. In spite of everything, Paul Haig was—you're gay, aren't you? I think I've heard about you."

"Yes."

"Have you ever loved a man? I mean, not just sex, but really had a deep love for that person?"

"Yes, I have. Most recently for the last nineteen years."

He looked at me sadly. "That's what I know now that I want. I thought I had it with Paul."

"His death must have been awful."

He shook his head. "Oh, I lost him before that, and *that* was awful. Paul was the love of my life, I thought—the first man I ever really gave myself over to. I had always been ashamed of being gay. I come from a family and a place where being gay is the most disgusting thing there is. That's why I could never accept my gayness and ended up with that asswipe Vernon Crockwell. But then I met Paul in Crockwell's group, and before long—I think the craziness of everything we were going through in Crockwell's program hit us at the same time and we started holding on to each other just to keep from going insane."

"That probably happens a lot in programs like Crockwell's."

"It happens a lot in Crockwell's own program," Bierly said.

"Dr. Crockwell's Inadvertent Dating Service. But for you and Paul things went awry after a while?"

"Paul was an alcoholic and couldn't control it," he said grimly.

18

"Like his mother is an alcoholic and his father was when he was living. That's basically what went wrong between us—Paul's drinking. He was sober at first, and going to AA. He'd been in the program off and on for a couple of years—much to Phyllis's consternation. She wanted him to drink, needed him to drink, and so sooner or later he did. It nearly always started up again after one of his lunches with Phyllis. Paul had some other problems too—lying was the main one. But his other flaws all had to do with his drinking, and his being gay, and his parents, especially Phyllis, whose boozy, twisted love was the kiss of death for Paul."

Although I wasn't sure, Bierly didn't seem to mean this literally.

He went on. "How the Haigs functioned at all is a mystery. When Paul was sober and he was being honest about himself and his family, he admitted to me what a mess they were. Lew, his father, was a real-estate developer who almost went to jail once in some kind of bid-rigging scheme. Paul said another time Mr. Haig got himself out of a financial fix he was in by blackmailing a rich senator, and he got caught at that too. Paul's father died of cancer, but cirrhosis of the liver would have killed him even if the cancer hadn't. Phyllis is in total denial about her alcoholism, and I think Paul's sister, Deedee, is probably alcoholic too. Paul tried—he really tried so hard—to be strong and honest and realistic about himself. But he couldn't. Maybe eventually he would have. But I couldn't take it after a while—the lying, the hidden bottles, the binges—and I gave up on him."

"Because he was screwing up your life too?"

"It got to be a matter of emotional, or maybe even physical, survival. Paul sometimes did some pretty crazy stuff when he was drunk, and sometimes I'd go along with it and regret it the next day. But mostly, I just couldn't stand not knowing which person he'd be from one day to the next. Finally, just after Christmas, when he really went off the deep end with a bottle in his hand, I got my own place and moved out."

I said, "The pros all seem to agree that in these unhappy situations you have to save yourself first. How did Paul react?"

Bierly shrugged. "He got drunk."

"I'm sorry it turned out that way. I hope you'll do better with the next man in your life."

He looked around to make sure we weren't being overheard. Then he leaned toward me and said in a breaking voice, "How could anyone think I killed Paul? Even that idiotic, deluded Phyllis—how could she *say* such a thing? I loved Paul. I couldn't live with him, and I couldn't be his lover anymore, but I still loved him. I could no sooner have killed Paul than—" Bierly looked nauseated at the thought—"than I could kill *anybody*. I'm just not a violent person. Oh, I have a temper. People will tell you. I can lose it, like a lot of people. But take another person's life? It's just not in me. I don't know if I could kill another person even in a war or in self-defense. So when Phyllis told the police I killed Paul and they called me in and questioned me—it just made me want to throw up."

I said, "But you don't think Paul killed himself."

"No."

"And you don't think his overdose was an accident either?"

"No, I don't think it was."

"Why not?"

"As for an accident, it wouldn't be like him. Paul was careful about pills. He never mixed drugs and alcohol. I was surprised when he told me he was on Elavil, just because any kind of drugs made him nervous. He didn't even like it when I'd smoke some weed or whatever once in a while. Alcohol was Paul's drug of choice."

I said, "And why not suicide?"

He shook his head emphatically. "Not a chance. Was Paul a nervous wreck? Oh, yes, poor Paul, he was one anxious son of a bitch—pun intended. He smoked too much, and he worked too hard, and the strain of trying unsuccessfully not to be the drunk his mother wanted him to be was brutal for Paul. But he coped. He found ways not only to survive but to function. He was a true Haig in that respect. And there's another thing: Paul had not only been on antidepressants and feeling relatively relaxed the week

20

before he died, but he hadn't been drinking either. I either saw him or talked to him on the phone almost every day, and I'd gotten to the point where I could tell if Paul had been drinking. He hadn't. He'd even started going to AA meetings again, he said."

The waiter, probably under corporate orders, was hovering, so I signaled for him and ordered a pizza of his choice. He said sausage and broccoli would be nice, and we said okay.

I asked Bierly, "With Paul's improved outlook, did you think there was a chance you and he might get together again?" More tentatively, I said, "Or did he think so?"

"Paul brought it up," he said, his voice going unsteady again. "As for us living together, I didn't want to. I told him I'd think it over, but I don't think I could have done it. At a certain point last winter—I can even remember the day—I realized I just didn't love Paul anymore in that way."

"Did you tell him?"

Bierly looked away and his face darkened. "No, I never did. When we separated at the end of last year, it was supposedly temporary—till Paul quit drinking permanently. But I guess I never really believed he'd stay sober. And one day I was sitting across from him at Queequeg's during Sunday brunch and he was talking about something unimportant—I have no idea what it was—and I looked over at him and I knew he would always be my friend but that we would never be lovers again."

"That happens to every couple," I said. "But it's usually just an attack of existential uncertainty, and it passes. Though this sounds different."

"It was," Bierly said. "I don't know about 'existential uncertainty,' but I know that with Paul, even though I still loved him, I'd lost confidence in him. And I didn't believe in us as lovers anymore."

"That feeling is always plain enough when it comes."

Now he looked sheepish. "I guess that's why when Paul died I didn't feel nearly as deep a loss as I would have a year earlier. I felt—I still feel—sad and hurt and confused. And I often miss

21

him. I just wish I could talk to him. Or touch him—God, we had such great sex together. That was a big part of the attraction and it's one reason I think I stayed with Paul as long as I did, even when he got to be impossible to live with. But mostly it's something else now that makes me miss him. I just want to sit down with Paul—I sometimes fantasize about doing it—and I want to ask him one question."

He looked at me steadily now, almost expectantly, as if I might ask the question myself—or somehow both ask it and answer it. I said, "What question would you like to ask him?"

He said, "Why did you die? How and why did you die?"

"Uh-huh."

"Who killed you? How did he do it?"

"You believe Paul was murdered."

"Yes."

"You seem so certain."

"I know Paul. Paul would not kill himself."

"Do you have any idea who might have done it? Who would have wanted to kill Paul?"

"I think I might know," Bierly said. "But first, let me ask you something."

"Okay."

"If you don't sign on with Phyllis Haig—and I don't think you will, because you seem too smart and too honest—will you let me hire you instead?"

"To do what?"

"To verify who killed Paul and have him charged and put out of business."

" 'Put out of business'—is that a euphemism?"

"Of course not. Just put in prison, which would get him out of the evil business he's in."

I said, "What if I investigated, and I succeeded, and it turned out Paul was murdered and the murderer was someone other than the man or woman you have in mind?"

He nodded. "I could live with that."

The pizza arrived. The waiter asked if we would like him to

22

serve the first slice. Bierly said no thanks. We served ourselves and went to it.

I said, "All other considerations aside, Larry, I'm not sure you can afford a private investigator." I told him my standard rate.

He grimaced. "That's a lot higher than I thought it would be."

"Phyllis Haig says you're rich. Your business was in trouble, but Paul left you his estate, and now you're flush with both his lucrative business and the rest of Paul's considerable assets. True?"

He chewed his pizza furiously. "What a load of Phyllis Haig bullshit crap," he said, bits of pizza flying from his mouth. His veins were pulsing again. "That woman. That *woman.*"

"Which part is inaccurate?"

"All of it is inaccurate. It was Beautiful Thingies that was in trouble, not Whisk 'n' Apron. Last year when Paul was drunk for most of two months, he had an assistant manager who robbed him blind and then disappeared. Paul got behind with the bank and asked Phyllis to bail him out. I'm not sure what he told her. It's conceivable he told her it was me who needed the money. Or he could have told her the truth and she just imagined it was me. The Haigs all lied to each other all the time, so none of them could ever believe what the other ones were saying. And with Phyllis, her brain is so atrophied from alcohol she can believe anything she wants to believe that fits into her warped view of people."

I said, "I can check all that out, you understand, about the finances. It would take me less than a day."

"I wish you would. And take what you learn and shove it in Phyllis Haig's stupid face."

"And Paul's assets?"

"He left me his '88 Honda, his household furnishings, his Abba tapes, and the three hundred twenty-two dollars in his checking account. He also left me his business, which was sixty thousand dollars late in payments on his business loan. When Paul died and I became executor and eventually beneficiary of his estate, the bank was about to foreclose on Beautiful Thingies. Paul

23

hadn't been worried about this—he told me a week before he died he'd come up with a way to pay off the bank debt. But the debt was still there when I took over, and I had to borrow myself up to the hilt to hold off foreclosure. So the fact is, for the foreseeable future Beautiful Thingies will be nothing but one big financial headache for me. Paul's estate is no place for me to go for liquid assets. Have I cleared that up for you?"

"You have." I chewed at the pizza, which was not Irish but hardly Italian either. It was rubbery and vaguely medicinal-tasting—Aleutian maybe.

I said, "Who do you think killed Paul, Larry?"

With no hesitation, Bierly said, "Vernon Crockwell."

"I had a feeling that's who you were going to say."

"Do you know him?"

"Only by reputation."

Bierly blushed. "I'm so embarrassed to admit that I actually went to him. But I was so fucked up and lonely in my personal life, and I thought—the thing is, I wasn't thinking at all. I didn't know much about homosexuality. I didn't even come out until I was twenty-five, and I didn't start to read intelligent books about it until I started with Crockwell and saw how crazy and unbelievable his ideas were and I went out and did some reading on my own. It was the same for Paul. Of course, he was in Crockwell's program under duress. From you-know-who. It's probably one reason she despises me to this day. Phyllis sent Paul to Crockwell to be de-queered. Instead, he met me and was queered for life."

"How long were you in the program?"

He blushed again. "I'm embarrassed to tell you. Over eight months. The program is supposed to run a year, and I came within four months of actually finishing it. Paul and I left the program last September ninth."

"It took you that long to figure out that Crockwell is a quack, or a con artist, or whatever it is he is?"

"It didn't take me that long. I was on to him within a couple of months. Paul saw through Crockwell too, though for a while he clung to the idea he might actually be straightened out—even

24

though we were happily fucking up a storm almost every night. Basically, he stayed as long as he did because of his mother, and I stayed until Paul worked up the courage to leave."

"And when you left the program, you and Paul left together?"

"That's right."

"Just toodle-oo out the door and that was it?"

"Well, not exactly."

"Uh-huh."

I waited. He chewed at his pizza and I chewed at mine. Bierly downed the remaining beer in his glass and then said, "Crockwell was furious when we announced one day we were well-adjusted homosexuals, thanks indirectly to him, and we were lovers and we were leaving the program. He started screaming how we were deluding ourselves, and we were going against nature, and we would always be miserable, and that's what we deserved. He screamed that we were disrupting the group, and for that we were going to be very, very sorry. He told Paul—this was in front of the entire group of ten guys—he told Paul that his mother would despise him for choosing to be a sexual deviant. Can you imagine a professional psychologist telling a patient something like that?"

"On this subject, yes, I can. Then what happened?"

"Paul pretty much told Crockwell—yes, *Paul* told Crockwell— to go to hell. Then we just got up and walked out. We were afraid we might feel a little guilty for a while, but we didn't. We rode the high for weeks that we got from walking out of Crockwell's office that day. We started going to gay rights events, even some political stuff, although I'm not really very political. I saw you at some of those political meetings, I'm pretty sure."

"I remember you too—and Paul."

"The high didn't last long, though. Paul went to see his mother and started drinking again. And everything went downhill fast. But that first month or so after we kissed Crockwell good-bye was the happiest time of my life, I think."

"You just said so-long and that was your last contact with Crockwell?"

25

"You got it."

"You or Paul never threatened him or attacked him? Or said anything that could be construed as a threat?"

"He threatened *us*," Bierly said, his color rising again. "He said we'd be very, very sorry for disrupting the group. But no, nobody threatened him that I can recall. We were just glad to be out of there."

"I'll bet."

"My real bitterness toward Crockwell—and Paul's too—was after we left, and we looked back on all the unnecessary pain he caused people. And is still causing. He's still in practice, if you can believe it."

I said, "Phyllis Haig says you assaulted Crockwell and threatened to kill him and Paul bought him off so he wouldn't have you prosecuted. Any idea what she was referring to?"

"Paul told her *that*? Oh my God!"

"That's what she said."

Blushing deeply again, Bierly said, "That is totally off the wall. It's obviously another one of Phyllis's bizarre, alcohol-induced fantasies. Either that or it was one of Paul's. When those two drank together—who knew what one of them would come up with."

I said, "You're blushing."

Bierly said, "I am?" and got even redder. "Well, I have to admit I'm embarrassed about a lot of what I've told you tonight."

"Uh-huh."

"It's not only highly personal, it's—I have to admit that some of the things I've told you about myself make me look pretty damn stupid."

"The blunders you've described to me are the kind a lot of us made at some stage of our lives. Are there other relevant blunders that you're not telling me about?"

"None that are relevant," he said, still blushing.

I said, "What makes you think Crockwell killed Paul? If Paul had no contact with Crockwell after last September ninth, what

26

would suddenly prompt Crockwell to homicide in March? I don't get that."

"Crockwell is a hater," Bierly said. "He carried poisonous grudges. In the group, he talked about other people who left, and he ranted and raved about how wretched they must be and how they deserve to be unhappy. He seemed to be obsessed with those people."

"But if he got satisfaction from their misery," I said, "he certainly didn't have to kill them."

Bierly blushed some more. I figured he was lying about some or much or all of what he had told me about his and Paul's departure from Crockwell's program and its aftermath. Yet he didn't seem to care if I thought he was lying. He just lied and blushed, lied and blushed. I didn't get it.

Bierly said, "Look, something deep in my gut tells me that Vernon Crockwell killed Paul. All I ask is that you investigate Crockwell and see what you can come up with. If I'm wrong, I'm wrong. But I don't think I am, Strachey." And then he brought out his checkbook.

4

"So which check do I cash?"

"Neer."

"What if Paul Haig was murdered?"

"Nnn."

"What if Crockwell did it?"

"Nnn."

"Are you falling asleep?"

"Mmm."

Spring stars twinkled over the Hudson Valley. We lay under a cotton blanket, cool, reasonably clean air moving west to east across us. Ted Koppel was our nightlight.

I said, "I'm more inclined to take Phyllis Haig's money because she can afford it. And as much as I like Bierly and sympathize with him—his instincts seem pretty consistently decent—his selective evasions are glaring and unsettling. There were moments tonight when if Bierly had been wired to a polygraph, he'd have registered at about an 8.6 on a Richter scale of liars. Of course, polygraphs are notoriously unreliable. The anxiety they detect can result from the emotional significance of the question asked as well as from the emotional significance of the answer given, or just from the stress of being questioned at all. Anyway, I do think Bierly lied about some topics—this from the man disgusted by alleged chronic Haig-family dissimulation—and I don't know why. Why might he?"

"Nnn."

"Phyllis Haig, on the other hand, is a serious drunk and a

deluded homophobe with hardly a rational thought in her head. Except one, maybe—that Paul was not suicidal. People can fool themselves about that, too, of course—parents, in particular, will sometimes deny their children's suicides in order to avoid facing what they fear is their own responsibility somehow. But the idea that Paul could have committed suicide was the one thing that seemed to generate an emotion in Phyllis Haig besides jealousy or outrage over deviations from the country-club norm. There was an emotional clarity to her assertions on this point that was lacking on others. On the other hand, even if she's right about Paul's not having killed himself, I could be risking my license and possibly my peace of mind—not to mention my shirt—simply by getting mixed up with this deranged heiress with friends in high places. I mean, not that my financial and mental survival should be the sole, or even chief, determinants in taking on a client, eh wot?"

"Zzzz." His breath, sweet with chicken tikka masala and Crest, was regular now against my chest, his arm limp across my midsection. I groped for the remote, found it, and zapped a murmuring Ted Koppel and a couple of nervous Clinton apologists into blackness.

I said, "Of course, the most interesting figure in all of this is the one I haven't talked to yet. Maybe I should meet Vernon Crockwell before I decide what to do. I doubt he'll be forthcoming on the subject of a couple of former patients, or happy to see me at all. But I've been curious about him for years, in a macabre sort of way, and now's my chance to both satisfy that curiosity and gather information that might help me make an important decision. What do you think, Timothy? Should I talk to Crockwell?"

He said nothing, but his breathing rhythm altered perceptibly and his shriveled member, sticky against my leg, seemed to throb weakly once. I took this to be a reply in the affirmative.

How could this be? I phoned Crockwell at 9:00 A.M. and told his machine I was a private investigator looking into the death of Paul Haig and asked for a few minutes of Crockwell's time at his convenience. At 9:55 Crockwell called back and, in a tone bordering on the cordial, informed me that he was extremely busy but that he could clear out a block of time at three that afternoon if that was convenient for me. I said it was and told him I would be happy to come to his office. I was eager for a peek inside Dracula's castle.

Why was Crockwell being so accommodating? When I phoned, I was fully prepared for a long wait before my call was returned, or for the call to be ignored, or for Crockwell to call back and explode with indignation. Instead, he was helpful and businesslike. Why? There had never been charges I knew of that Crockwell's treatment program was anything but voluntary, that he lured unsuspecting homosexuals into his lair and forced them at gunpoint to feign excitement over nude photos of Ole Miss sorority aquacade contestants. So when I drove out to Crockwell's office in mid-afternoon I felt reasonably safe but still mystified.

He had a suite in a sixties-suburban business block off Western Avenue near the Stuyvesant Plaza shopping center. His listing on the building's directory just read "Vernon T. Crockwell, Psychologist, Suite 508." I took the elevator up and found a door with a sign that gave Crockwell's name and said "Enter Here." The fluorescent-lit, windowless waiting room had a blue couch and two blue chairs with a shiny washable finish and a table stacked with old copies of *People*. Crockwell apparently figured there would be plenty of opportunity in the rooms beyond this one for overstimulation.

On the wall opposite the couch, a mirror was mounted. I stood before it and carefully mouthed the words "You're pretty fucking intrusive, Vernon," and within seconds a door opened behind me.

"You are Donald Strachey?"

"Yes—Mr. Crockwell? Or is it Dr. Crockwell?"

"Please follow me, Donald."

He didn't look like Bela Lugosi, but he'd never have passed for John Denver either. He was tall and fiftyish and grave, with a narrow, lined face, a beak of a proboscis, and what I sensed was a lot of muscle tension. He looked as if a good neck rub might have improved his outlook, but I didn't offer him one.

Crockwell led me on a brisk, wordless hike along a corridor past three closed doors and one that was open. I caught a glimpse of a big sunlit room with a dozen or so plastic chairs arranged in a circle. I followed him around a bend and noted that the nearly bald spot on the back of his straw-colored-turning-gray hair was bigger than mine but smaller than Timmy's. Crockwell's brown sport coat was wrinkled in the back, a sign of an important man who sat in a chair.

"Sit down, Donald," he said in his stern, avuncular way, indicating where I should do it. Behind a broad, uncluttered fake-mahogany desk, Crockwell manhandled a black leather swivel chair into position and lowered himself into it. The bookshelves on the wall behind him were crammed with clinical texts published by companies like Uplift House and the Yolanda Schnell Foundation for Sexual Normalcy. Leaning on one shelf was a framed degree, or diploma, with Crockwell's name on it from the North American Psychosexual Institute of Moline, Illinois.

To Crockwell's right was a window overlooking the shopping center. The window was shut, probably unopenable except with a wrecking ball, though the odor of deep-fried chicken nuggets had permeated the suite from somewhere below and hung in the still air. It seemed an unlikely atmosphere for considering people's sexual appetites, or any other kind. But that could have been the point.

"Now I want you to tell me, Donald," Crockwell said, as if he were the school principal and I had been sent to his office, "who it is you represent in your investigation of Paul Haig's suicide. Are you working for a member of Paul's family, Donald?"

"I'm sorry, Vernon, but I can't tell you that," I said, and he peered at me stonily. "But what I can tell you, Vernon, is that I've spoken with two people independently who knew Paul quite well and doubt that he committed suicide. He seemed to have been anxious over some work problems a little earlier, but he'd

31

been on an antidepressant for several weeks before his death and by at least two accounts was feeling relatively chipper. The coroner's verdict appears to have been the result of a too cursory, perhaps even slipshod, investigation."

"I see, I see." He screwed up his face and shifted uneasily.

"And since Paul was a client of yours, Vernon, it seemed to make sense for me to cover all the bases and get your input on his emotional makeup, if you wouldn't mind helping me out on this. Paul was your client as recently as eight months ago, I'm told. I realize that patient-therapist confidentiality is sacrosanct in your profession, Vernon. I respect that. It's important in mine too. But since Paul is deceased, would it be possible for you to contribute to my investigation of his death by revealing to me the nature of the mental problems that first brought Paul to you as a client?"

It occurred to me as I said this that it wasn't just morbid curiosity that had brought me to Crockwell, or any real hope that he might immediately shed light on Paul Haig's death; what I most wanted was to poke at Crockwell with a stick and see if he'd try to snap off my leg with his powerful jaws. He didn't, but he bristled a little, and said, "If you're an investigator worth your salt, Donald, I'm sure you know perfectly well why Paul Haig was my patient. I work with the sexually dysfunctional."

"You mean gay people."

"Yes."

"And Paul had come to be de-queered."

"Made whole, brought into sync with nature, yes. Please don't bait me, Donald. It was no trouble for me to find out that in addition to being a private investigator you are a well-known gay libber around Albany. If you would like my opinion on Paul's emotional state as it might relate to his death, I will give it to you. But I'm not going to waste my time and yours debating aspects of the human personality you obviously know nothing about." He sat looking smug, though not quite 100 percent certain I wouldn't lunge at him. He kept one hand out of sight at all times below the desk—though if he had an alarm button down there, or a firearm,

32

or a little squeeze toy that might suddenly go "Fuh-wee-too, fuh-wee-too," I had no way of knowing.

I said, "It is Paul Haig's death I'd like your views on, Vernon, but I want you to realize that I am quite willing to be convinced that I am a freak of nature. I always try to keep an open mind about that. Do you have scientific studies showing that your theories are correct and the results of your therapy beneficial?"

Still keeping his hand out of sight, Crockwell said, "Yes, innumerable studies have been completed, Donald. And the human testimony is voluminous and incontrovertible. Tens of thousands of formerly sexually damaged men and women who have found wholeness and fulfillment through therapies such as mine have even organized socially and politically. They call themselves the ex-gay movement. I'm sure a man of the world like yourself, Donald, must have heard of it."

"Yes, I've heard about 'ex-gays,' Vernon. I've also read about the ex-ex-gay movement, made up of people who claim therapy such as yours is a pathetic snare and a delusion. They say ex-gays are people who live out their lives and try to behave in a way that denies their deepest and truest natures, and that people who remain in the ex-gay movement are either vegetables or liars."

Crockwell had undoubtedly heard all this before and appeared unfazed by it, though still cautious enough to keep his trigger finger poised. He said, "I have no need, Donald, to debate this matter further with you. You claim to have an open mind, but it's obvious that you do not. I would like to point out to you, however, that nature does not produce homosexuals. Why would it? Nature produces heterosexual males and females capable of mating and with an impulse to do so. In the sexual maturation process, something goes awry in some people. But this unnatural sexuality can be corrected. Are you old enough, Donald, to remember the song 'A-doin' a-what comes naturally'?"

I looked at him, not sure I was hearing what I was hearing. I said, "I've heard it. It's from *Annie Get Your Gun.*"

He said nothing more, just looked at me as if he had delivered the clincher in his argument and it would be foolhardy of me to

33

attempt any reply. I said, "Vernon, I've heard of psychologists going to Freud for their theoretical underpinnings, or to Adler or Sullivan or Erik Erikson. But Irving Berlin? This is a first."

"You're missing the point, Donald. A long time ago you decided to miss the point, and there's nothing I can do about that—unless, of course, you decide that you want me to."

I was growing increasingly queasy in Crockwell's presence—and a little puzzled too. Was this magisterially patronizing but mild-mannered twit the raging monster Larry Bierly had described to me just a day earlier? The man who—when Bierly and Haig announced they were leaving Crockwell's group—purportedly screamed that they were deluded, and they'd be miserable and sorry, and that they were disturbing the group, and Haig's mother would hate him forever for being a sexual deviant? Was this a distorted impression of Bierly's, or a total lie, or what?

I said, "Vernon, one of the people I've spoken with about Paul Haig is Larry Bierly. You remember Larry, of course."

He blinked and his face both tightened and colored. "Yes, I remember Larry Bierly all too well."

"He told me that when he and Paul became lovers and left your group together, you blew up. He said you ranted and carried on and screamed that they would be very sorry for leaving and for disrupting the group. Does any of that ring a bell?"

Now Crockwell was blushing—*blushing*—just as Bierly had. Looking as if he were trying not to break into a stammer, or get up and rush from the room, Crockwell said, "That is a gross exaggeration, Donald—a serious, serious exaggeration of what actually transpired. Did I try to impress on Paul and Larry that they were making a terrible mistake? Of course I did. Did I lose control and act in an unprofessional manner? Absolutely not." Now his face was as red as a new Miata.

I said, "Vernon, did Larry Bierly ever threaten you in any way? Or attack you?"

Most of the blood in his body now seemed to have surged up and pushed against the front of his face. He said, "Oh, no. No attack, and no threat that I can recall."

34

"Bierly never threatened to kill you?"

"I'm sure I would remember if he had done that, Donald. I would have notified the police, in fact. Tell me, is it Larry Bierly who hired you to investigate Paul's death?" His breathing was shallow now, but I had no intention of performing mouth-to-mouth resuscitation on Crockwell. Let him die.

I said, "My client wishes to remain anonymous for now. I can neither confirm nor deny that it's Larry Bierly, or that it's anyone else, or that it's not anyone else. Sorry."

"But you're going to pursue the killer?" He brought both hands up on the desk now and folded them tightly in front of him. His respiration was still poor, and his knuckles were as white as his face was red. Not good.

"To tell you the truth, Vernon, I'm not sure that I am going to do that. I'm making some preliminary inquiries and then I'll decide if I think it's worth my client's money for me to keep spending it by digging into this. Say, did you say 'killer'? Did you ask me if I was going to pursue Paul Haig's 'killer'?"

"Why, yes."

"So you don't think Paul committed suicide? Or that his death was accidental either?"

He tensed up even more. "I—I don't know. But this seems to be a theory that's going around. That Paul Haig was murdered."

"What do you mean by 'going around'? Are you saying you heard it before I walked in here today?"

"Yes," he mumbled, and nodded once.

"Who from?"

"The Albany Police Department." Now sweat broke out around his eye sockets.

"When?" I asked.

"Yesterday. They asked me to come to their office at Division Two. There was a Detective Finnerty and a Detective Colson. They—I have to tell you, it's very difficult for me to admit this, Donald—but they seemed to think Paul Haig might have been murdered. And, they seemed to think that I might have done it. They were not explicit, but the implications were clear."

35

"Where did they get an idea like that?"

"Someone had sent them an anonymous letter suggesting that I killed Paul. The letter was accompanied by a tape cassette of part of a therapy session of the group Paul was in. On the tape, I made some comments that could be interpreted as angry. Or perhaps even threatening."

"I thought you said your words and tone were always professional and controlled."

"Of course, absolutely. But on this one occasion, particular things I said could conceivably be misconstrued by the lay observer."

"Or by a jury, I suppose."

He didn't like the sound of that and came out with a little "Oh."

"Did they play the tape for you, Vernon?"

"Yes."

"Who made the recording? Did you, Vernon?"

"Oh, no, no, Donald. That would be unethical without first obtaining the permission of the patients. No, the recording must have been secretly made by one of the members of the therapy group."

"Uh-huh. Maybe one of the members whose opinion of your ideas and methods fell off at some point. Were there others in the group besides Paul Haig and Larry Bierly who ended up considering you a demented crackpot?"

With effort—I could all but hear his sphincter grinding—he said, "I wouldn't know. All the members of that group have moved on. I haven't been in touch with any of them. It's always possible one or two of the ten men in the group were insufficiently motivated and later slipped back to their unnatural ways. And instead of blaming themselves, they blamed me. That can happen."

"I'll bet it does. Did the cops give you a copy of the tape?"

"No."

"Did they ask you for an alibi for the night Paul died?"

He loosened up just enough to slump in his seat. "Yes, they did."

"Did you have one?"

"No."

"Too bad."

"I'm here alone Thursday nights, Donald, often until after midnight. I go over my notes of the past week and transfer them into my computer. Those solitary Thursday nights in this office are extremely valuable to me and I protect them—cherish them, I can say. So regrettably I have no alibi for the night of Paul's death."

"Well, what the cops have is little to go on. Unless something more solid turns up, it's not at all likely they'll charge you with anything, Vernon. They're just fishing around. So, did you kill Paul Haig?"

He slumped some more and said quietly, "Of course not." Then, the strain of it all showing again, he gave me a funny, embarrassed look and said, with obvious effort, "My attorney, Norris Jackacky, tells me that you are quite capable, Donald."

"Thank you."

"Although a police investigation would end up clearing me of any role in Paul Haig's death—if word went around that I was even a suspect in a former patient's murder, the harm to my reputation would be incalculable. Faith and confidence are the coin of the realm for a psychotherapist."

"Oh, I thought it was seventy-five or a hundred or a hundred and fifty dollars an hour."

"You're being facetious and I'm sure you know what I'm saying, Donald. If doubts about my character circulate, my effectiveness could be compromised, even wiped out. And my wife, my family—we could be ruined! I can't let that happen." He looked at me grimly, and before he said it, I heard it coming. "If your other client decides not to pursue the investigation of Paul Haig's death, Donald, I would like to retain you to carry on the investigation on my behalf. I can pay you whatever the other client would have paid, or more if that's necessary. It may feel somewhat odd to you to be working for me. But the arrangement would be independent of our positions on sexual and other matters. It would be purely professional—a business transaction, much as either of us might conduct with an accountant or a dry-cleaning establishment."

Crockwell reached down to where his hand had been earlier, but instead of coming up with a pistol or a rubber ducky, he produced a checkbook.

5

I'm amazed you actually met with Crockwell," Timmy said. "Wasn't that premature?"

"You thought it was a good idea last night."

"I did?"

"You were a little groggy."

We were at the dining-room table at the house on Crow Street. He'd brought home a Vieille Ferme 1991 and had grilled a nice slab of bluefish, and I was responsible for the salad and the Tater Tots.

"You aren't actually considering taking that madman's money, are you? You've had some reprehensible clients over the years, but surely Crockwell is beyond the pale."

"I'm not going to take anybody's money until I've got a clearer picture of what the possibilities are in this. For one thing, I want to talk to the cops and see what they've got. Phyllis Haig, Larry Bierly, and Crockwell have all fed me stories that have their dubious aspects. I'm especially mystified over conflicting accounts of threats that Bierly and/or Haig may have made against Crockwell, and vice versa, and a possible assault by Bierly on Crockwell. In those areas, all three of them are antsy and unconvincing."

"Maybe the tape will clear some of that up. Will the cops let you hear it?"

"They will if they think I can be helpful. Otherwise they'll poke me in both eyes with sticks and leave me standing in the middle of Washington Avenue during the morning rush."

"You've survived worse from the Albany Police Department."

"I have to admit I'd love to take Crockwell's money, but I'd also like to see him put out of business. And if a homicide charge, however false, accomplished that—hey, it must all be part of a larger plan. Let his missus, who's a Sunday-school teacher in Loudonville, he says, till the Crockwell fields for a year or two while he goes somewhere and gets deprogrammed."

Timmy gave me his never-entered-the-priesthood-but-still-a-Jesuit-at-heart look. "I don't think you mean that."

"Of course I do."

"Don, Crockwell is a dangerous quack and should be exposed as such. And an enlightened public should scorn and discredit him and make it clear to one and all he's bad, not good, for the health of anybody's mind and soul. And I certainly hope that you don't accept a nickel of his soiled pelf. But being wrongly accused of taking a life is a fate nobody deserves."

"Look, if he didn't do it, the chances are slight that he'd actually be convicted and sentenced and hung by his thumbs."

"Sure, slight."

"Timothy, if there is any such thing as evil in what passes for the civilized world, this guy represents it. He's a kind of Mengele's-pale-shadow for the nineties, performing weird experiments on people's sexuality for the sake of an ancient, barbaric prejudice. Should fate suddenly turn around and perform a weird experiment on Vernon Crockwell's reputation—well, it's all in the game."

"Are you really talking about fate, or fate with a little nudge from you?"

"I'll just follow the question where it leads. You know me. Pass the Tots, please."

"Yes, that is the way you operate, usually. And it's one of the things I most admire about you, when I do." He passed the mooshed-potato balls. "How does Crockwell do whatever it is he does to his clients? Is it the talking cure, or aversion therapy, or what?"

"I didn't ask and I'm not sure I want to know. Group therapy

40

is part of it—I've got a list of the eight other men in Haig's and Bierly's group—but I got the impression from Bierly there's more to it than that. Crockwell's suite had one big conference-type room that I saw. There were a number of closed doors, too, but I don't know who or what was lurking behind them."

"Crockwell gave you a list of his clients? Isn't that unethical—or even illegal?"

"He couldn't, he said, even though he's convinced, probably rightly, that someone in the group is out to get him—nail him as a murderer, whether he is one or not. At my suggestion, though, Crockwell was willing to sit quietly and examine his white knuckles while I phoned Larry Bierly, who was happy to provide me with the names and biographical sketches of each of the group members. Two others besides Haig are dead, it turns out—a double-suicide leap from the Patroon Bridge in February that was witnessed by six motorists and doesn't look suspicious, just sickening. It sounds like a kind of indirect murder. Anyway, Bierly said that all or most of the seven surviving group members probably considered Crockwell capable of actual murder and would be willing to testify to that effect, giving examples of his behavior that led them to this harsh opinion."

"I remember reading about the bridge suicide. What a horror Crockwell is—true-believerism at its most destructive."

"Crockwell, of course, affects the stance that all the group members except two adored him. And since Paul Haig is dead, Bierly is his prime suspect for secretly taping a therapy session and sending the tape to the cops. It was funny, though. I had to drag it out of Crockwell that Bierly was logically the culprit if the others in the therapy group were Crockwell's diehard fans. He gets very uncomfortable when Bierly's name comes up and seems to hate to have to think about him at all."

"Did you tell Crockwell that Bierly is trying to hire you to pin the supposed murder on Crockwell?"

"That didn't come up, no. Nor did I tell Crockwell that Phyllis Haig wants to hire me to pin the supposed murder on Bierly."

"This is getting complicated, Donald. What if this entire crew is nothing more than an extended nest of paranoiacs and revenge seekers? Can you afford to spend a lot of time mucking about in this with no payoff either in the form of justice or cash?"

"Somebody will pay me—there's no reason to be concerned about that. Offers keep pouring in. It wouldn't surprise me if Jerry Falwell called up and wanted me to verify that on the night he died Paul Haig was seen leaving the Howard Johnson's Motor Lodge on Route 9W with Hillary Clinton. If I can show that Haig wasn't murdered, Crockwell can pay me. If I can show that Haig was murdered and Crockwell did it, Bierly can pay me. If I show that Haig was murdered and Bierly did it, then Phyllis Haig can pay me. As I see it, it's a no-lose situation."

Bypassing the jar of tartar sauce I'd brought out to improve the Taters, Timmy squeezed some more lemon on his remaining savories and said, "With the people you've described to me who are involved in this, Don, a no-lose situation sounds out of the question. I've got a feeling about all of this that's not good."

"I'll just have to be at my nimblest," I said. "Like this—"and proceeded to juggle three Tater Tots, Barnum & Bailey-style, until two landed in my lap and one in Timmy's wineglass.

6

Mum, poker-faced Detective Lieutenant Al Finnerty had taken over the APD homicide unit after longtime head Ned Bowman's surprise early retirement and relocation to semirural Tennessee. This followed an incident at a Democratic Party hotel-ballroom fundraiser where Bowman's presumably speculative but overly jocular description of the mayor's mistress's genitalia was overheard by His Honor, who had stepped behind a column momentarily to zip up his fly.

And just as Bowman had been one of the public loudmouths of Albany, always ready with a crude opinion or a piece of nasty advice for citizens who fit into categories he didn't like—"fairies" headed his long list—Finnerty was one of the city's officers who was almost pathologically closemouthed. He had learned too well that whatever his views on public or private matters, large or small, the nineties comprised a decade for never, ever expressing any of them.

Finnerty's reticence was in some ways refreshing after Bowman, whose mouth was a running sewer. But it made it hard to get any information out of Finnerty at all. His saving grace, however, was this: he was lazy. And it was possible to obtain information, occasionally even assistance, from him if he could be convinced that his cooperation with a private investigator—even a "controversial" one, as he liked to call me—might reduce his workload by an iota.

"I'd like to help you out, Strachey," Finnerty said at 8:03 Friday morning, "but I don't know much about Paul Haig's death, and I

43

haven't had an opportunity, really, to give it a great deal of thought."

We were in his office overlooking Arch Street and the old South End, urban-renewed into oblivion in the sixties by Nelson "the Visigoth of Tarrytown" Rockefeller and only just beginning to recover. Finnerty's coffee mug was a plastic job from a chain donut shop, whose logo, facing me, was as close to an open display as Finnerty would ever risk. His most naturally forthright disclosure was a product placement. He sat across from me, his doughy face devoid of interest or curiosity. I was somebody to put up with for a time, and then I'd go away, and that was fine—unless a way somehow emerged for me to do Finnerty's job for him.

I said, "What about the coroner's report, Al? The conclusions are all public information anyway. How about saving me a trip over there?"

"Glad to help you out, Strachey. It was suicide. Suicide was the ruling. The coroner is experienced in these drug-and-alcohol fatals, so I'd be inclined to go along with his judgment on that. Coroner Bryerton is an old hand at these tragedies."

"Then why did you have Vernon Crockwell in here yesterday badgering him about where he was on the night of Paul Haig's death? Do you think Haig's 'suicide,' as you're calling it, was medically assisted, or what?"

Finnerty did not exclaim over this, but he did betray what might have been thought with a barely discernible dilation of his left pupil. "Is Crockwell your client?" he said.

"I can't tell you who my client is. But I saw Crockwell yesterday and he told me about the anonymous letter and the tape full of threats, so-called, and your pestering him for an alibi, one of which he hasn't got."

"Our interview with Crockwell was routine," Finnerty said. "When an accusation of homicide is made, we check it out."

"And?"

"And we did."

"And you still think Haig's death was suicide?"

44

"Maybe."

"Uh-huh."

He looked at me and I could see through his eyes and into his brain, which was weighing whether, if he opened up a little with me, I might make his life harder or easier.

Finnerty said, "Crockwell doesn't look like a killer to me. He's a doctor and a very conservative man."

"Sure," I said. "A member of the nonhomicidal classes."

"Anyhow, Strachey, the coroner's verdict is in. A determination of suicide in the death of Paul Haig has been duly rendered. That's official."

"Yes, but is it correct? I think that's what we ought to be talking about here, Al, what with your dragging citizens in off the street for close perusal. Even if they are citizens like—*especially* if they are citizens like Vernon T. Crockwell, famous local psychologist."

His brain was squirming in its little cavity, but he said—mumbled really—"I will tell you this, Strachey: that there was something funny about the circumstances surrounding Paul Haig's death."

"Such as."

"The officer who was first on the scene reported it—mentioned it to me later, is what I should say."

"What was that, Al?"

He said, "The pill canister containing the Elavil that was mixed with alcohol, and that killed Haig, had its childproof lid back on and tightly attached and put back on Haig's bathroom sink. But the pathologist determined that Haig was already very drunk when he consumed the pills that turned out to be fatal. If that's so, then how did a drunk replace the childproof cap on the canister and put it back in its place? Getting one of those caps back on when you're stone cold sober is hard enough. Do you follow me, Strachey?"

"Yes, I do."

"It might be nothing, it might be something. But it's interesting."

"It sounds like something to me, Al. So, how come the coroner's verdict was suicide, what with this question unresolved?"

"The coroner didn't know about the pill canister," Finnerty muttered. "It wasn't in the detective's written report because he didn't put it in."

"A serious error."

"No, just a breakdown in communications. It happens, Strachey. To err is human. We all make mistakes. The situation now, however, is this: if I reopen the case and go charging away, I make either the department or the coroner look incompetent. There's not a chance in hell I'll do either, which I'm sure you can appreciate. But of course if *you* happen to make the coroner look stupid—hey. You're just that fag detective that I can't control, what with the Constitution and all that. Are you still with me, Strachey?"

I said, "Sure. I do your job for you, including taking all the risks, physical and financial, and then you call me names in public. It's irresistible. Count me in."

He nodded. "You're not recording this, are you?"

"I wish I were."

"No, I don't think you do."

"Al, I'll take your word for what I wish or don't wish. Does anybody else besides me outside the department know about this snafu?"

"No. And if I read this in the *Times Union* tomorrow morning, you can kiss Albany goodbye, U.S. Constitution or no U.S. Constitution."

"That's fair enough. You questioned Crockwell, Al, but I understand that Phyllis Haig, Paul's mother, has her own suspicions about her son's death, but she doesn't think it was Crockwell who did it. She's landed on Larry Bierly, Paul's old boyfriend. I guess she came in here hyperventilating, and then you went chasing after Bierly too, huh? To ask him where he was on the night of Haig's death."

"Again, routine."

"And Bierly had an alibi and it checked out?"

46

"Yes, it did. He seems to be in the clear. Is Bierly your client?"

"I'm not at liberty to say, Al."

"Or is it Mrs. Haig? Or even Crockwell? Not that I could imagine him hiring an avowed homosexual."

"I can't say. You know how PI clients like their privacy. Anyway, lots of people hire homosexuals. If we all suddenly quit our jobs and emigrated to Norway, every business and occupational pursuit in the nation would be utterly decimated, except for nerve-gas manufacturing and chain-restaurant interior design. But I see your point. I can't tell you if Crockwell is or isn't my client, but I can say that I have spoken with him and I have his permission to hear the tape you received anonymously in the mail."

Finnerty said, "That tape is not Vernon Crockwell's property. His voice is on it, but the tape is the property of the Albany Police Department."

I hoped that was all pro forma bluster. I said, "Do you want me to sign something? Slip you a fifty? What's this about? You said you could use a little help on this and I'm willing to provide it. All I ask is discreet access to whatever you've got that's pertinent. Is that unreasonable?"

"We'll get to that," he said, and he looked suddenly somber, almost intelligent. "Strachey, when did you last see Larry Bierly?"

"Wednesday night, out at Millpond. We shared a pizza over his dinner break. Why?"

"You haven't been in touch with him since then?"

"I spoke with him briefly on the phone yesterday afternoon. Why do you ask? Have you been in touch with him?"

"In a manner of speaking, I have."

"Uh-huh."

His eyes narrowed and he said, "I guess you really don't know. Around eleven o'clock last night someone shot Larry Bierly in the Millpond Mall parking lot."

"Oh, hell."

"He's in serious but not critical condition over at Albany Med

47

with gunshot wounds to the chest and neck. Didn't you hear the news this morning?"

"I listen to public radio. WAMC would only report a shooting if it took place on the floor of the legislature or in a box seat at Tanglewood. Just how serious are Bierly's wounds?"

"He's in no real danger. He was lucky, and the last I knew they were saying he'd recover completely."

"Is he conscious?"

"Not yet, so far as I know. Bierly had surgery at midnight. Guy Colson's over there now to see if he can get a statement."

"Is anybody in custody?"

"Not yet. We're checking our snitches, but this doesn't look like robbery—Bierly's watch was on him when he was found, and his wallet with eighty dollars in it. Another mall employee, a waitress at Scarf-It-Up, finished her shift at eleven and went out to her car in the lot designated for employee parking. She found Bierly wounded and unconscious next to his car, with his keys on the tarmac beside him. The EMT crew was on the scene within six minutes. Their best guess is, Bierly had been shot within fifteen minutes of when they got there. Unfortunately, no witness has come forward. It's pretty quiet out there at that time of night. We do have a couple of people who were coming out of the cinemas on the other side of the mall around ten till eleven, and they think they heard shots, but now they aren't sure if the shots they heard were outside the mall or in the movie they'd just seen. They said it had a lot of shooting and explosions. That's as much as I can tell you for now, Strachey, because that's as much as I know."

I said, "This is bad."

"But the question now is, Strachey, do I know as much as you know about this incident?"

"Come again?"

"What's your connection with Bierly? If he's not your client, is he a friend of yours?"

"Al, I can't say, one way or the other, whether Larry Bierly is or is not my client. I can tell you that he is an acquaintance."

Finnerty let something he may have meant as a human expression form on his face. He said, "Boyfriend?"

"No, I have one at home."

"I mean on the side."

"Oh, I see what you mean. No, not that either. Do you have a woman you see on the side, Al? You're married, aren't you?"

"This is not about me, Strachey," he said, and blushed.

I said, "This is not about me either, Al. Mainly it's about Paul Haig, and now it looks as if it may be very much about Larry Bierly too. Look, if I'm going to perform the work Albany's taxpayers are paying you to perform, I'll have to have something more to work with. First, I need to see the letter you received accusing Vernon Crockwell of murder, and I need to hear the tape that came with it."

"I could arrange that if I wanted to," he said inanely.

I asked, "Is Crockwell a suspect in Bierly's shooting?"

"Like I told you, Strachey, we have no suspect in the shooting."

"Last night was Thursday night. That's Crockwell's no-alibi night. Have you talked to him?"

"I'm seeing him in an hour. You said you talked to Crockwell yesterday yourself. Did you tell him that Bierly was trying to hang a murder rap on him?"

"I didn't mention it, no."

"What did you tell him?"

"That I thought he was a crackpot, that he ought to be tarred and feathered by the mental health profession, stuff like that. I was there solely to ask him questions about Paul Haig."

"I guess you think Larry Bierly's shooting is connected in some way to Paul Haig's death. Am I right about that?"

"It's hard to say, Al, for now. Let me see the letter and hear the tape, and then I can start clearing this case for you—or cases, as the case may be."

Two for the price of one, he must have been thinking, the price of one being zip. Without speaking he got up and left the room. I watched the motor traffic on Arch Street and the pedestrians strolling to work or school under a spring sun that smiled down on all the people.

Finnerty came back with a sheet of paper and a cassette player and placed these on the desk in front of me. Then he left the room without a word, closing the door behind him.

7

The paper appeared to be a photocopy of the original. It looked like a computer printout, with no date and no return address. It read:

> To the Albany Police Dept. Homicide Division:
> Paul Haig died on March 17th. Verdict, suicide. Wrong.
> Ask Vernon Crockwell, the so-called psychologist,
> where he was that night. Crockwell had his reasons for
> shutting Haig up. Play this tape. Vernon Crockwell has
> gotten away with murder, so far. Justice demands that
> you look into this. Let justice be done.

There was no signature. Was this Larry Bierly's voice? It sounded more like Phyllis Haig's voice than Bierly's. But she thought Bierly, not Crockwell, was responsible for her son's death, and she wouldn't have been siccing the cops on Crockwell.

I pressed start on the cassette player. The sound quality was poor, the voices distant and tinny, but the words were discernible. I got out my pad and made notes while the tape played:

"Now, Larry, it is customary to discuss the reasons when making a decision to terminate therapy." This was obviously Crockwell, Mr. Unctuouser-Than-Thou. "I think you'll agree that you owe it both to the group and to yourself to present your reasons for termination and see if we all think it is wise. How do you feel about that?"

51

"You mean if *you* think it is wise." I recognized Bierly's voice. "Don't give me that what-the-group-thinks shit, Crockwell—it's always been what *you* think and it always will be."

A voice I didn't know said, "Now, Larry, all Dr. Crockwell meant was—"

"All he meant"—this was Bierly again—"was that you're a bunch of sick fucks, and sick fucks like you had better do what the doctor says. But you're not sick and I'm not sick, and the only thing that's sick is all of us deluding ourselves and coming here every week and trying to turn ourselves into people we're not. We're not straight, we're gay. That's all there is to it. And it's not because our fathers weren't affectionate with us or some crazy shit like that. We've been over and over that. Hardly any American fathers are affectionate enough with their sons, but it doesn't make them homosexual, for God's sake. Nobody knows why we're gay. We're all different and we all come from different kinds of families—"

"That's not true!" Another new voice. "The patterns are obvious. If my parents had—"

"Hey, Lar, don't you remember why you joined the group?" Yet another voice I hadn't heard. "Don't you remember how all alone you felt after you did it with another guy? How you always hated yourself in the morning? Do you want to go back to that kind of life?"

"But, Gene, I know now that that's not the only choice—"

"Perhaps," Crockwell said, "we should hear from Paul. I know that you and Larry have become good pals, Paul. What do you think of Larry's decision to close off therapy and terminate his relationship with the group?"

Now came a long pause filled with scratchy electronic presence but no words. Then a quiet voice that must have been Paul Haig's said, "I'm leaving too."

A stir now, with murmurings that were indistinct except for one clear "Oh no" and a loud "Oh my Lord Jesus!"

Then a brief silence, followed by Crockwell's "I can hardly believe my ears—that you would even consider disappointing the group by doing such a thing, Paul. Or disappointing your mother."

"He's not just leaving," Bierly said. "Paul is leaving with me. Paul and I have been dating each other for some time now. We love each other deeply and we are going to have a life together. It's—it's great what we have—security and peacefulness. The one really good thing about this group is, it brought Paul and me together. We became friends and then lovers—well, to be honest, we became secret fuck buddies, and then friends, and then lovers. And now we're going to be—life partners, and neither of us have ever been happier in our lives, or ever imagined that we could be this happy and fulfilled."

"There is no peace and love in a lake of fire!" someone boomed—the one who had yelled "Oh my Lord Jesus!" before—but the others quickly shushed him up.

Then, after a little silence, Crockwell said coldly, "Paul, can this be true? That you too subscribe to the illusion that Larry has embraced so emotionally without being cognizant of the consequences?"

"No—no, I think Larry's right," Haig said. "I'm just—gay. I always was and I always will be, and there's nothing wrong with that. The one thing I do know is, I love Larry. When we're together, I just feel—like Larry said—peaceful."

"Peaceful?"

"Well—yeah."

"But how long does this feeling of peace last, Paul? One minute? Five minutes? Do you feel peaceful when you and Larry walk down the street together? When you're with your mother, or when you think of her?"

"No, but that's because—"

"It's because of people like you, Crockwell!" This was Bierly again. "You and your bullshit that you spread around that there's something wrong with gay people. What's sick is you making us sit in those rooms looking at pussy and zapping us when we look at dicks—*that* is sick. All you ever did for me was make me sick of looking at pussy. I never cared about women's bodies one way or another until I came here, and now I can't stand the thought of them."

"Why do you think that is, Larry?" This was Crockwell, trying to sound oh-so-cool, but with tremors creeping in. "When you, ah, think about, ah, a woman's genitalia, what comes to mind?"

"I think of *you*, Crockwell, and I think of those dungeons down the hall—those electrocution chambers that are like something you read about that Saddam Hussein does to people in Iraq. And I'll bet the same thing is true for everybody in this room, isn't it? The only time you ever think about heterosexual sex is when you come here and get strapped into Crockwell's electric chair. Admit it—isn't it true?"

"No, no, that is definitely not true!" This was a voice I'd heard once before, briefly exclaiming indignantly over Bierly's assertion that nobody knew why anybody turned out gay. With the inflections of what can only be termed a real screamer, this group member again exclaimed, "Because of Dr. Crockwell's procedures, I have finally gotten in touch with my normal sexuality, and I resent your implications in regards to my manhood, Larry! You can just—speak for yourself!"

"Dean, you should be ashamed of yourself," Bierly said. "I mean—suing your own mother and father because they made you gay? I never said anything before, because I never thought you'd go through with it. But that has to be the dumbest, greediest, meanest thing I ever heard of somebody doing to their parents. And Crockwell, you never discouraged him. You—"

"I am not suing them for the cash!" Dean screamed. "It's to set an example for others, and you know it!"

"Larry," Crockwell said, "there's something about Dean's anger with his mother and father that you feel quite strongly about. Would you like to talk about that?"

"No, I'd like to talk about you, Crockwell, you evasive, manipulative piece of ignorant shit! You always throw it back on each of us, but it's you who's everybody's problem. How'd you like a dose of your own medicine? What comes to mind? How do you feel about me challenging you? What if I dragged you down the hall and strapped you in one of those chairs and zapped you every time you looked at—whatever the fuck turns you on? How do you feel about that, Crockwell? Tell us about your mommy and daddy. What did they do to produce such a cold-blooded, sadistic piece of crap? Huh? Huh?"

"Now, Larry, you *are* being disruptive." Crockwell was asserting himself as the voice of authority, but it was coming out croaky. "Now, we do have rules to follow as to disruptiveness— rules we all agreed to follow."

"If that's the way Larry feels, I think he should just leave!" This was Mary Mary Quite Contrary again. "The rest of us are here because we want to be here, and to help each other act like real men are supposed to."

"Dean, a real man stands up for himself and stands up for what's right. A real man doesn't turn his life over to some—some Nazi lunatic."

"You are telling *me* what's a real man, Larry? Now I'm sure I've *heard—it—all.*"

"Those are strong words you're using, Larry," Crockwell said. "You seem to have some awfully strong feelings about me and my role in the group. Perhaps it would be helpful if you examined those feelings."

"Or perhaps it would be helpful if I put your lights out, just put you out of business, Crockwell! A year from now—or even a month from now—everybody in this room with half a brain would thank me."

"I just think maybe Larry ought to leave if he's going to talk like that." This was the one called Gene again. "One of the main reasons we're here is to not let our behavior be ruled by our emotions. If you can't control your emotions, Larry, then maybe you better go. What you're saying sure does get in the way of the things we're trying to accomplish here."

"Gene, what are you trying to accomplish? I remember you said when the group began that you wanted to stop considering yourself a freak. But turning yourself into a gay married liar or a eunuch—isn't that the worst kind of freak of all? Because it's not really you. What every one of you are doing here is trying to make yourself live a lie. You're all paying Crockwell to turn you into liars. Is that what you want to be? A bunch of lying assholes?"

This caused a largely indecipherable uproar, but it was Crockwell's voice that rose above the others and went on when the hubbub subsided. "That is quite *enough*, Larry. That is enough vulgarity, and name-calling, and—and—disruption. There are rules here—*rules!*—and you are breaking the rules. I want you to *stop* it."

"Fuck you, Crockwell. Fuck you and fuck all your fucking control-freak rules. Paul and I are out of here, and if the rest of you poor fucks want to stay here and let this—this Saddam Hussein torture you—well, I feel sorry for you. I just feel sorry."

"Paul, your mother is going to be so disappointed in you—so very, very disappointed. To reject her, to turn your back on her—"

"Will you please just shut up about my mother!" Haig snapped.

Bierly said, "The only thing that interests you about Phyllis Haig, Crockwell, is that she paid Paul's fees on time."

"Your father's heart would be broken if he knew," Crockwell went on. "Now that your mother needs a normal, whole man in the family more than ever, you plan to tell her your intention is to remain half a man. And that you're proud of it yet! You're going to rub her nose in it!"

"What are you saying?" Haig moaned. "Now that my father is dead, I'm supposed to marry my mother? What are you talking about?"

"Now, Paul, I never said—"

"Larry, you're right about him! You are so, so right about him!"

"Paul, this discussion involving your mother seems to arouse strong feelings on your part. Wouldn't you like to talk about those feelings?"

"Damn it, just you keep my mother out of this. My mother doesn't need a lot of ugly and depressing shit like this. My mother is a wonderful woman, full of life, who always does her damnedest to look on the bright side of things. She's got *joie de vivre*. She's like Auntie Mame. To her, life is a banquet and she lives it to the hilt. Yes, she's set in her ways. But I'm used to that. She's not going to change, but why should she? Mother and I got along just fine before she sent me here, and we'll get along just fine after I leave. So, just—just don't bring Mother into this, Dr. Crockwell. Mother has absolutely nothing to do with this! Do you hear me? Do you understand what I'm saying?" Haig had become shrill and sounded as if he was losing control.

"Your mother despises homosexuals," Crockwell said evenly. "That is the hard fact of the matter that you are leaving out."

"Crockwell, you are scum!" This was Bierly. "You are a dangerous, dangerous man—"

"Homosexuals are scum!" Crockwell shot back. "Homosexuals spit on nature and morality. Paul's mother understands that. In his heart, I believe, Paul does too. I'll have to speak with your mother, of course, Paul. I'll have to explain to her that the tough love she exhibited when she brought you to me will have to continue if you choose to leave the group. That it will have to take other forms, and I can advise her about that."

"Dr. Crockwell," Haig said, "I wouldn't do that if I were you. Do not bring my mother into this."

"Oh, it would be a matter of professional responsibility. I would be remiss if I failed to advise your mother, Paul."

"If you turned my mother against me," Haig said, very calmly now, "you would be very sorry you did."

"Oh, I don't see how."

"Don't do it."

"Are you threatening me, Paul?"

"I am telling you. Do not come between Mother and me."

"It's your sexual deviancy that's a barrier between you and your mother's love and approval, Paul. Not I."

"Just stay out of my family, Dr. Crockwell."

"Fortunately for you, in the long run, Paul, I can't do that."

"Well, I'll stop you. I'll just—stop you."

"You'll what?"

"I mean it, Dr. Crockwell. I'll do what I have to, to stop you from coming between Mother and myself."

Now came a long silence. Chairs shifted. Finally, in a voice strained as never before in the session, Crockwell said, "No, you won't stop me, Paul. If I have to, I'll stop you. If you get in the way of my carrying out my duty to uphold moral standards of normalcy, I'll stop you, Paul. I'll just stop you dead in your tracks."

There were gasps and ohs and ahs, and then the tape went silent. I listened to the silence for a minute, then fast-forwarded to the end of the sixty-minute cassette. The remainder was blank. I flipped the tape. The other side was blank in its entirety.

I pocketed the photocopy of the anonymous letter suggesting that Vernon Crockwell had killed Paul Haig, along with my notes on the contents of the tape. I left Al Finnerty's office and went down the stairway and out into the pale sunlight.

I'd left my car up near the house on Crow Street, and that was okay. I didn't need to examine my feelings about where I'd parked my car. Strolling over to Albany Med would give me a chance to air out my brain cells, which had been polluted by my visit of some minutes via the tape with Vernon Crockwell and his victims, or his collaborators, or some unhappy combination of the two. But victims in what? Collaborators in what? Except for the obvious—a quack operating abusively as a mental health professional—I did not yet understand what was happening here.

8

Bierly was still unconscious following his surgery, his condition serious but stable. I got just close enough to him to see that a hospital security guard was posted outside his door. When I asked the charge nurse whether Bierly had had visitors, she said a police detective had come and gone and a friend of Bierly's was out in the waiting area. A man named Steven, she said.

A family of Punjabis occupied the corner of the waiting room near the television monitor, peering with interest at Joan Lunden. Across the room from them, glowering out the window, was a sturdy, well-built man in faded jeans and a flannel shirt. His age, fortyish, suggested the flannel was not hip-kid mosh-wear but was a relic of the butch-gay seventies. He wore work shoes that looked as if they had actually been worked in, and he had a ruddy, angular Anglo or Saxon face and thick auburn hair that curled over his collar. He could have been Lady Chatterley's gamekeeper, Mellors, except for the sweetish cologne that became apparent as I approached him, and the look of hostile suspicion the man gave me as I introduced myself. Mellors, an enduring object of erotic fantasy of mine since the summer between my senior year in high school and freshman year in college, would have been delighted finally to meet me, I'd like to have thought, but this guy clearly wasn't.

"Donald Strachey? No, Larry never mentioned you." He gave my extended hand a brusque tug but didn't get up. I sat down beside him and he shifted uncomfortably.

"The nurse said your name is Steven."

"Yes, it is."

"And you're a friend of Larry's?"

"Yes, I am."

"I guess you're pretty shocked and upset, Steven."

"Of course I am."

"Are you two old friends?"

He stared at me.

I said, "I'm a private detective."

This got a look of mild alarm that was quickly replaced with something that looked calculatedly neutral. He said, "How do you know Larry?"

"On Wednesday he told me he wanted to hire me."

"Hire you? What for?"

"It has to do with the death of Paul Haig. Was Paul a friend of yours too?"

A sheen of perspiration was visible now on his upper lip. His scent was getting stronger too, less perfumy, more Mellors-like. He said, "I didn't know Paul. I mean, not all that well."

"His death was ruled a suicide, but Larry thought Paul was murdered. He never mentioned that to you?" He just stared at me, closemouthed. "It seems odd, Steven, that Larry wouldn't have mentioned it to someone who was close enough to him to visit him in the hospital first thing on the morning after he'd been shot."

This shook something loose. "Well, he did mention that he had some suspicions about Paul's death. But Larry never said anything about hiring a detective or anything like that."

"How long have you known Larry?"

"Not long."

"A year? Six months?"

"About six months."

"Where did you meet?"

He glared. "That's no concern of yours. What right do you have to ask me these questions?" Then he thought of something that made him wince. "Are the police going to question me too?"

60

"There was one here this morning, a detective by the name of Guy Colson. I guess he missed you. You'd remember him."

"I just got here about twenty minutes ago. I heard on Channel 8 that Larry had been shot, and I drove straight up. There would be no point in me talking to the police. I don't know anything about who shot Larry. Wasn't it probably a robbery or something?"

"It doesn't look that way. Nothing obvious was taken. Why don't you want to talk to the cops?"

"Because—because I have nothing to offer. I have no information." Sweat rings were evident now under his arms. "I have no idea who would want to shoot Larry."

"What about Vernon Crockwell?"

"Oh, no." He blanched—not blushed, blanched—and shook his head three times.

I said, " 'Oh, no, Crockwell would never do such a thing,' or 'Oh, no, it must have been Crockwell who did it'?"

"I have to go," Steven said. He stood up abruptly and strode toward the corridor.

I followed. "What's your last name, Steven, in case anybody has to get in touch?" He said nothing, just turned in the direction of the elevators. "Where do you live?" He marched down the hall in what looked like a barely controlled state of panic. He worked at the elevator down button repeatedly, as if it were a suction pump and his exertions could make the doors open and the car appear. I stood next to him and waited. When a car finally showed up, I stepped inside with him.

An orderly was on board behind a tiny ancient woman in a wheelchair. "What's that smell?" she said. The orderly made a sniff-sniff face but didn't reply. The two of them got off on the third floor. Steven and I rode down to the first. He watched the floor numbers light up and didn't look at me.

As he moved quickly out the main front door and cut right toward the visitors' parking lot, me breathing hard at his side, I said, "Steven, what are you afraid of?" His pace quickened even more. He said nothing.

"Maybe I can help you. Larry trusted me, and you should too."

He looked frantically this way and that, trying, it seemed, to remember where he parked his car.

"Are you in danger, Steven? If you don't want to get mixed up with the police, you can talk to me and what you say can be between us." He spotted his car and made straight for it. "I think Larry would want you to talk to me, Steven. When he regains consciousness, he'll talk to me anyway, so let's get a head start on this thing, whatever it is. Let's make sure you don't get hurt, and that nobody else does."

He shook his head once desperately and said, "You don't want to know." Then he unlocked the door of an old black VW Rabbit with mud spatters on the side, got in, slammed the door and locked it, made the engine cough, backed out, and headed for the exit gate. I might have followed the VW if I'd had my car with me. But it seemed sufficient to note the Rabbit's license number, which had a code not for Albany County but for Greene, the next county down the Hudson Valley.

I hiked down New Scotland Avenue and across Washington Park. The city had spruced up the park's cozy shady glens and ample sunny greenswards for spring strollers and loungers. Rank upon rank of canary-yellow and plum-colored tulips lined the walkways, each tulip no doubt a dues-paying member of the Albany County Democratic Party. In the last election, many of them had probably voted.

At my office on Central, I hiked up the window to let some air in and must out. Another chunk of old caulking fell off the pane, so I ran a couple of feet of duct tape along that edge to prevent the decapitation of any of the winos who had come to regard my entryway as a place of late-evening safety.

My machine, more up-to-date than its surroundings, had recorded three calls. The first said: "Hi, this is Larry Bierly calling Thursday night at nine-fifteen. I was just wondering if you'd made a decision about working on investigating Paul's death. Please let me know. I'm at Whisk 'n' Apron till about eleven. Then

I'll be home, and then I'll be back here about noon tomorrow. I'm eager to hear what you think, and I really hope you'll take the case. Vernon Crockwell should not be allowed to get away with murder. Thanks."

Bierly had been shot just two hours after placing this call. He did not sound apprehensive, as if he had learned anything startling since I'd met him the evening before. I'd checked the machine from home not long before Bierly's call. But even if I'd gotten the message, it was unlikely I would have told him anything that would have prevented his walking out to the farthest reaches of the mall parking lot and being gunned down just after eleven. Nor could I have informed him that I had decided to hire on with him, or not to, for I had made no such decision on Thursday night. And I still hadn't. I needed to know more.

The second call on the machine went like this: "Don." This carried a tone of reprimand and was followed by a breathy pause. "Don, thissus Phyllis Haig. You never got back to me, Don." Another pause, as if she might be expecting my live or recorded voice to respond. "Well, fine then." More heavy breathing. "Don, are you there? Are you gonna pick up?" Now came a couple of sharp bangs and some scratching sounds, as if she had dropped the receiver. Soon she was back. "Hey, are you gonna take the cake—take the case? Or aren't chu? Don, you gotta get that Bierly cocksucker. That fairy has gotta pay. I'll make him pay for taking my Paul away from me. I'll—" The receiver hit something and fell again, but after more fumbling I was left with a click and a dial tone.

The third call was from my other potential client. "This is Vernon Crockwell calling, Donald, at eight-twenty-five A.M. Friday. Please contact me at your earliest convenience. Larry Bierly has been shot and seriously injured, and the police apparently regard me as a potential or actual suspect. They are on their way here to interrogate me now. I don't know which is more harmful to my reputation, Donald, the police being seen entering my office or my being seen at the police station.

"Donald, I've been in touch with my attorney, Norris Jackacky, and he has repeated to me his opinion that in spite of your misguided and ultimately futile lifestyle you are the most capable private investigator in Albany. You can probably take some satisfaction in knowing that you've got me over a barrel, and I'm in no position to hold your deviant sexuality over you. We can discuss sexuality later, if you prefer. In any case, please call me at my office to discuss this more urgent matter at your earliest convenience. Thank you."

I had a quick flash of Crockwell "over a barrel," where he was "in no position" to hold my deviant sexuality over me. Could he be . . . ? No, almost certainly that wasn't it. Arch-homophobes did occasionally turn out to be homosexual psychopaths. There had been at least one gay-bashing congressman caught with a call boy, and countless reactionary men of the cloth who couldn't keep their hands off hitchhikers or altar boys. And of course there had been J. Edgar Hoover railing against the commie-homo menace whenever he wasn't off-duty with Clyde Tolson rhumbaing in a darling cocktail dress at the Stork Club.

But for Crockwell to have devoted his entire professional life to the relentless exorcism of gay men's sexuality while he was secretly gay himself wouldn't have been just sick, it would have been monstrous. Not that some gay men—Roy Cohn, probably Hoover—weren't monstrous. It was always a possibility. As was deeply repressed homosexuality that sometimes surfaced in the form of horrified fascination with gay sex and the urge to stamp it out. But that was getting into realms beyond me—in most cases probably beyond anybody's sure grasp.

What did seem certain, though, was some kind of odd, powerful connection among Crockwell, Haig and Bierly—and possibly "Steven" and others—that went beyond what I knew or had overheard on the tape of Haig's and Bierly's last session with Crockwell's cure-a-fag group. If so, then what was this connection, and was it somehow getting people killed? It was time to learn more about the other members of the therapy group.

9

First I phoned a friend whose business runs credit checks and asked her to find out all she could about Paul Haig's and Larry Bierly's business and personal finances. She said she'd report back to me in a day or two.

Then I called a contact at the Department of Motor Vehicles and learned that the mud-spattered VW Rabbit was registered to Steven St. James, with an address in the town of Schuylers Landing in Greene County. I noted this and retrieved St. James's residential phone number from what used to be called, descriptively, New York Telephone but now is called—as if it were a nasal decongestant—NYNEX.

Fifteen minutes after leaving a message, I got a callback from a psychotherapist friend in Westmere who specialized in actual sexual dysfunction. As I suspected, she was familiar with Crockwell's practice; she had even treated a few of his alumni. I learned that unlike open-ended groups whose members came and went at various times, Crockwell's was a set one-year program that included both group therapy and individualized aversion therapy. He always had three groups going, each meeting once a week at different times. One old group ended and one new group formed every four months. This way, men who had queued up to be de-queered would never have to wait too long to get started. (Lesbians wishing to be un-dyked were referred to a similar program run by a colleague of Crockwell's in Schenectady; my therapist friend, a lesbian, informed me that the

Schenectady program included not only group and aversion therapy but also hairstyling and makeup tips.)

Then I got out the list Bierly had provided me—and whose accuracy Crockwell had, in effect, confirmed—of the ten men in the previous calendar year's therapy group. The first two men on the list were Haig, now deceased, and Bierly, unconscious in the hospital. Two others were known to be dead, Bierly had told me: Gary Moe and Nelson Bowkar had fallen ill with AIDS-related infections soon after the group had concluded in December and both had died in early February, a double suicide. Bierly had heard later that the two had secretly been lovers while in the Crockwell therapy group—it's where they met—and they had remained in the group because nineteen-year-old Bowkar's family had begged him to stay, and twenty-year-old Moe's evangelical church had paid his $8,200 per annum nonrefundable fee to Crockwell, and Moe didn't want the congregation to think its money had been wasted. Bierly said there had been nothing suspicious about the suicide; Bowkar and Moe left anguished, profusely apologetic notes to their families and jumped off the I-90 Hudson River bridge together.

That left six. Grey Oliveira was married, lived in Saratoga, and was described by Bierly as one of the more stable and rational members of the group, but hard to take on account of his sarcasm. Bierly called Roland Stover, of Albany, a guilt-ridden religious zealot and "fucked-up something awful." LeVon Monroe and Walter Tidlow, also of Albany, were best buddies, Bierly said, and he suspected that they were more than that. Eugene Cebulka, of East Greenbush, was a nice guy, Bierly said, and generally sensible and with a good grip on reality; Bierly wasn't sure why he had stayed in the group.

Bierly had described Dean Moody as "a lunatic." Moody had initiated a lawsuit against his parents, Hal and Loretta Moody of Cobleskill, alleging that through their recklessness—Loretta's emotional closeness to her son and Hal's emotional distractedness and uninvolvement—they had turned Dean into a wretched homosexual. This one I had read about in the *Times Union* earlier

in the year, when the Moodys, all three of them, had been sched-
uled to appear on Montel. Now I was sorry I hadn't tuned in.

Bierly I didn't need to track down, and luckily the others from
the therapy group were listed in area phone books. Conve-
niently, and probably more than that, Monroe and Tidlow shared
both a number and an address on Allen Street. Only one group
alumnus was at home when I called; Walter Tidlow said his
"roommate" LeVon would be home at lunchtime and they would
be willing to discuss Crockwell vis à vis Haig vis à vis Bierly if I
wanted to drop by. He also offered lunch; I hadn't yet accepted
anybody else's offer to foot my expenses, and I happily took
Tidlow up on his offer of free food.

I phoned Crockwell at his office and got his machine. Finnerty
and Colson were probably going at him. If Crockwell had stuck
to his schedule, he'd have been alone in his office Thursday night
when Bierly was being shot, and therefore alibiless. Which meant
Crockwell was in trouble whether he had shot Bierly or—as now
seemed more and more likely to me—not. Crockwell's accustomed method of assassination was subtler. The tape someone in
the group had made and sent to the cops showed that Crockwell
could lose control. But losing control when provoked was one
thing, and premeditated murder (Haig) and attempted murder
(Bierly) was far more dire. It was easy, though, for me to keep an
open mind on this point. I had next to nothing to close it around.

Not enough time had passed for Steven St. James to get back
to Schuylers Landing, so I didn't phone him. Anyway, what else
could I say to him? St. James was scared to death of something,
and calling him up and making vague ominous noises would
only spook him more. I figured I'd drive down there over the
weekend. The Hudson Valley in May actually looked the way
Church and Cole and the other local romantic painters of the last
century had imagined it, dramatic and dreamy, with De Millean
sunsets and enormous blue vistas that made people look tiny but
lucky to be alive for a wistful little spell in the Empire State.

I almost returned Phyllis Haig's drunken call of the night
before, but couldn't quite make myself dial the number. She

67

would put her foot down and give me a piece of her mind and tell me a thing or two about manners whenever she got hold of me, but that would have to wait.

Tidlow and Monroe shared the top floor of a tidy, well-kept two-family house on South Allen Street. The stairs up to it were carpeted in Astroturf and the inside of the apartment was stuffed with antimacassared Victorian-style reproductions and shelf upon shelf of carefully arranged and recently dusted glass bric-a-brac. It wouldn't have surprised me if Amanda Wingfield had sashayed into view.

Instead, I found two hospitable men in their mid-thirties who had laid a lovely table and served me Campbell's tomato soup, always a way to this man's heart, and a plate of Ritz crackers with butter. This was washed down with Price Chopper cola. It's easy to tut-tut at the cuisine of the lower middle classes, but I had a feeling Tidlow and Monroe could have eaten better if they hadn't each spent $8,200 the previous year on Vernon Crockwell's de-sodomization program. Or maybe they served this food because they liked it. I know I did.

"We saw about Larry getting shot on the TV this morning," Tidlow said, "and we just couldn't believe it. We never knew anybody who got shot, even though it's extremely common nowadays. American society has become so violent."

"What a tragic year it's been for Larry. First Paul commits suicide, and now this horrible incident. Our hearts go out to Larry."

"You don't think Larry shot himself, do you?" Tidlow said.

I said, "He was shot twice, once in the neck and once in the chest."

"Oh, that's right. I guess it would be hard to shoot yourself more than one time. I shouldn't have stumbled on that one. Me, who never misses *Murder, She Wrote.*"

"Did Paul shoot himself?" Monroe asked.

"No," Tidlow said, "that was pills and liquor, like Marilyn."

I nearly asked if Marilyn was another acquaintance of theirs

68

who had died, but caught myself. Tidlow was a balding, pleasant-faced, pale-skinned man who worked as a bookkeeper for the company that owned the Millpond Mall. He said he'd seen Bierly at the mall occasionally—as he had Paul Haig when he was alive—but hadn't spoken with him in recent weeks and had left the mall at eight P.M. on the previous night, three hours before Bierly had been shot.

Monroe was a balding, pleasant-faced black man who was a bookkeeper for the state tax department. He wore a tartan-plaid necktie and matching socks. He told me he was originally from Rome, New York, where he was named after his mother's favorite pop singer, Vaughn Monroe.

Tidlow was due at the mall at two and Monroe was on his lunch break, so I tried to move the conversation along. "Were both of you there the day last year when Paul and Larry left the therapy group?"

"Who told you LeVon and I were in that program, if you don't mind my asking?" Tidlow said.

"Larry did. I spoke with Vernon Crockwell, but he would never mention any names, if that's what you're worried about," I said.

They glanced at each other. Monroe said, "No member of the group was ever supposed to reveal to outsiders who the other group members were. It was strictly confidential. But I must say it's entirely agreeable to make an exception in your case." He gave me a sly look and winked.

"The thing of it is," Tidlow said, "we heard something about you." He gave me a sly look and winked too, and I gave them both a sly look and winked back at each of them.

"When you called," Tidlow said, more at ease now, "you said you were investigating Paul Haig dying, but you didn't say who was employing you to do this." They both looked at me with curiosity, and I saw some older, wiser version of myself looking at me with curiosity too.

I said, "I am not able to reveal to you at this point in time exactly who my client is. But I can tell you that a number of

69

people connected with Paul Haig consider his death suspicious. That's why I'm interested in the last therapy session that Paul and Larry took part in."

"Suspicious in what way?" Monroe said, buttered cracker poised in midair. "You mean perhaps it wasn't suicide?"

"Despite the official verdict, there's a question in some people's minds."

"Golly," Monroe said.

Tidlow said, "This is the first time I heard about that. My word."

"Paul was always a pretty unhappy camper," Monroe said. "So when I heard he committed suicide I wasn't all that shocked. Now somebody thinks—what? He was murdered?"

"Yes."

"My heavens," Tidlow said.

I said, "That's why I'd like to get your take on that last therapy session they participated in. I understand some remarks were made that some of those present regarded as threats."

"They do? Why?" Monroe asked. They both looked confused.

Tidlow said, "Whose opinion is that?"

I said, "Didn't Crockwell kind of lose it at that session? That's one account I've heard. Crockwell told Haig he'd regret leaving therapy and he'd upset his mother, and then Haig warned Crockwell not to bring his mother into it or Crockwell would be sorry, and then Crockwell said if Haig tried anything funny Crockwell would stop him dead in his tracks. Do you remember it any differently?"

Tidlow said, "That sounds right, but there was more to it. Later on, Dr. Crockwell said he was simply using a therapeutic technique to get Paul to bring his feelings out so he could talk about them, and he apologized to the other members of the group for pretending to lose his temper."

"I see. And did this explanation and apology come before or after Paul and Larry left the room?"

"It was afterwards," Monroe said. "I know because I think it was I who asked Dr. Crockwell if he was going to call up Larry

70

and Paul, if they really didn't come back, and apologize to them."

"What did he say?"

"He said he sure would."

I said, "Crockwell was quite the manipulative fellow."

"Oh, he took the cake when it came to manipulation," Tidlow said. "But does somebody think he killed Paul? That sounds far-out."

Monroe said, "Dr. Crockwell didn't need to kill anybody in the group. He was already cutting off their whoosy-whatsis, figuratively speaking. That seemed to be good enough for him." Tidlow nodded sagely in agreement, and I did too.

I said, "You both seem to have come out of therapy with a low opinion of Vernon Crockwell. Would you care to say more on the subject?"

"To be perfectly frank," Tidlow said, "LeVon and I are both of the opinion that Dr. Crockwell is either deeply misguided or even, conceivably, a fake."

"In addition to being some kind of depraved sadist, like a monster in a Stephen King novel," Monroe said. "Let's not forget that."

I said, "But you stayed in therapy with him anyway? Or did you come to these negative conclusions later on, after the course of therapy ended?"

Tidlow said, "I stayed because my mother paid the eighty-two hundred dollars for the program in advance, and because I met LeVon there and I wanted to keep him company. I faked it, even went to all the 'private sessions'—that was Crockwell's euphemisms for the zap routines—and even managed to get a boner, if you'll excuse the expression, looking at pictures of *Playboy* bunnies. Even though I had to rub my weenie raw to do it. Does that answer your question?"

"That's vivid enough. What about you, LeVon? How come you stayed?"

"To prove to my ex-wife that it wouldn't help. That I was gay and nothing could be done about it. And the same goes for me—

I could get through it because Walter was there. We figured if we could survive Vernon Crockwell together, we could survive anything."

They both grinned at me across their empty soup bowls.

I said, "I guess that wasn't the effect Crockwell was after."

They chuckled. Monroe said. "On our twenty-fifth anniversary we're going to have a big dinner at the Luau Hale over in Pittsfield, where Walter's from, and make sure Crockwell is invited."

"You two seem to be as comfy and well-adjusted as most of the gay men I know," I said. "I don't suppose the same could be said of the other members of the therapy group."

"Are you going to talk to them too?" Tidlow asked.

I said yes.

"Then you'll see for yourself. Some are compos mentis, and a couple of them are the most addlebrained people you'll ever meet in your life."

"Which ones are which?" I asked.

"Gene and Grey are compos," Monroe said, "but Roland and Dean are out in la-la land."

"Would you say either Roland or Dean is dangerously demented?"

Tidlow said, "I'd say they might be dangerous, wouldn't you, LeVon?"

"Oh, my, yes."

I said, "Both of them?" They nodded emphatically. "What makes you think they might be dangerous?"

"Well," Tidlow said, "Roland believes that homosexuals who don't repent should either be stoned to death or thrown over a cliff. And Dean thinks they should be locked up in state mental hospitals. I'd say that makes them rather dangerous."

"Especially if they got elected to something," Monroe said.

"Is either of them running for office?" I asked.

Monroe said no, he didn't think so, and I wondered if either Roland Stover or Dean Moody had found cruder outlets for their hatred of homosexuality.

I said, "To your knowledge, did any member of the therapy

72

group ever record one of the sessions, either openly or secretly?"

They stared at me. Monroe said, "No—why? Did somebody tape us? That would certainly be untoward."

"It's just something I'm trying to track down. Does the name Steven St. James ring a bell with either of you?"

Tidlow said, "I never heard of him. Who's he? Any relation to Susan Saint James of *Kate and Allie?* That was one of my favorite shows. I have all the tapes."

"I don't know yet who he is," I said, "or what his connection is to any of this. When I asked him about his involvement, he just said I didn't want to know."

"It looks like you do, though," Monroe said. "I hope when you find out, you aren't too shocked."

I said no, I hoped I wasn't.

10

Back in the office, I dialed the numbers I had for the other members of the therapy group but got only one answer. A woman at Grey Oliveira's number in Saratoga said I could reach him at work in Albany in the State Division of Housing and Community Renewal. Oliveira took my call, and when I told him I was investigating Paul Haig's death he agreed to meet me at five at a bar on Broadway. He said he too had been surprised by Haig's suicide, and he'd wondered if there hadn't been more to it.

I tried Crockwell and got his machine. It was just past two in the afternoon, so I didn't know if he had been led off to jail or if he was busy attaching electrodes to the limbs or genitalia of his current patients.

Again, I started to dial Phyllis Haig's number but couldn't quite make myself hit the final digit.

I did reach Al Finnerty, who said he'd heard from the hospital that Larry Bierly was improving steadily. Bierly was barely conscious but still too drugged up to be interviewed. The doctors had told Finnerty maybe Bierly could talk and make sense in a day or so. Then, presumably, he might be able to identify his attacker, or, if he got a look but it wasn't anybody he knew, he could at least provide a description. Finnerty asked me how I was coming with my own inquiries. I said I still hadn't learned much of coherent substance, which was an awkward but true fact.

Grey Oliveira was short and muscular in the conservative dark suit and gaudy multicolored tie that somebody had decreed must be worn by men under fifty working in offices that year. He had a well-sculpted Mediterranean face, oldtime-matinee-idol wavy black hair, and big liquid gray eyes it was hard not to gaze into in a more than businesslike way. Despite a certain awkward salty ache I was feeling, I was sure I hadn't given anything away when—about sixty seconds after I walked up to him—Oliveira said, "You're gay, aren't you?"

"I am. What tipped you off? Was it the spitcurl or the Barbie lunch box?"

"Just something about the way you were looking at me. Or not looking at me. Or looking at me and looking as if you'd be a lot more comfortable if you were looking at somebody else. It's my eyes, I know. Gay men and straight women find my eyes hypnotic. This goes way back—to infancy, as a matter of fact. My parents were the first ones to be smitten. I was named after my eyes, as a matter of fact. And these eyes have done extremely well for me over the years."

"I'll bet."

"Only up to a point, though. People don't tend to come back for seconds. The problem is, I've got bedroom eyes but a dick the size of a thimble."

"I'm sorry to hear that."

He laughed once and shook his head. "Hey, can't you tell when somebody's pulling your leg? Sheesh." He winked at me and raised his glass of beer.

I said, "Are you bisexual? Or are the straight women whose gaze is sucked into your limpid pools not so lucky as all those gay men?"

"One of them is," he said, gazing at me. "I'm married. In fact—hey, why am I telling you this? You wanted to talk about Paul Haig's suicide. That's why we're meeting like this. And here I am instead regaling you with the raunchy details of my sex life."

"I haven't heard any raunchy details," I said, "and I guess I don't need to. But the general outline of your sex life does interest me. I'm trying to get a clearer picture of Crockwell and his therapy groups, especially the one you were in."

"Oh, you don't want to talk about my dick, then?"

"No." All around us other men were drinking draft beer and palavering about the young baseball season, and the market, and the legislative session, and how Clinton was in trouble and how he deserved it because he was a wuss and a liar and a phony: the boomers devouring one of their own.

Oliveira said, "Don't get me wrong. I'm all talk. I'm a happily married man. For me, as the song goes, there's no fiddle-dee-dee. In fact, you might say, I'm twice faithful, doubly married. Do you know what I'm talking about, Strachey?"

"I haven't got a clue."

"I've got both a wife and a boyfriend," he said, and sipped his beer. My bottle of Molson arrived and I imbibed from it. "Up in Saratoga, we are très civilized. None of your bourgeois narrow-mindedness in our hip precincts. I love my wife and I like my fuck buddy, and I need what they both have to offer—her comfort and security and good home, and his stiff one. It's a full life."

"I guess it could be."

He grinned. "I might sound a little flippant about my cozy arrangement, but don't misunderstand me. I really am lucky. Annette is the love of my life and I couldn't live without her. My boyfriend is in a similar situation and it all works. Both of us get to keep the marriages we value, and so do our wives, who are cool with the deal. They know exactly where we are and who we're with when we're not home—a claim most wives are unable to make about their husbands. And it's all AIDS-proof too, a closed circle no virus can penetrate—unless it turns out AIDS can be picked up through overexposure to the sheets at Stan and Ellie's Mountain View Motel on Route 9. Then I'm in trouble."

"It does sound safe, if underly romantic."

"I lost interest in romance a long time ago. I never had much luck with it."

76

"Uh-huh."

"Not with men, anyway."

I said, "Is that why you ended up in Vernon Crockwell's therapy group?"

He grimaced into his beer, then looked up at me disgustedly. He said, "I did that for Annette. I never expected it to work and I don't think she honestly expected it to either. But this was before I met Stu, and I was getting pretty antsy going without dick—the whole AIDS thing had scared me off of men completely—and Annette heard about Crockwell and thought if I went to him I could get my craving for men exorcised and find peace. Get a gay-sex lobotomy or something."

"Sounds grim."

"You'll never know how grim it was."

"And you met Stu while you were still in the group?"

"I met him last summer, at a Little League game. How's that for family values?"

"Commendable. You've got kids?"

"Bobby, ten, and Ellen, eight. Both nice kids too."

"And you and Stu were in the Little League bleachers and your eyes met and bells rang and violins played?"

He said, "I told you, that's not how it works with me. I've never been in love with a man. Basically, I just like sucking cock."

"Your life may lack romance, Grey, but not intellectual honesty, I guess."

At this, he simply gazed at me a little sadly.

I said, "You said on the phone you were surprised that Paul Haig had committed suicide and you thought there might be more to it than met the eye. How come?"

He sipped his beer. "Paul wasn't the type to kill himself. He was the type who'd escape from life in easier ways."

"Like what?"

"Like alcohol."

"He did have a history."

"He was weak. Taking his own life would have required a

degree of strength I never once saw in Paul Haig."

"But he walked out on Crockwell," I said. "That certainly took will."

"He followed Larry Bierly out. That's all he did. By the time they left, Larry had more sway over Paul than Crockwell did, that's all it was. Paul was a drunk and a weakling. People like that don't kill themselves. What they do is, they die slowly from their addictions and they make other people's lives miserable while they're at it."

"You seem to know a lot about the subject, or have strong opinions about it anyway."

"Both," he said. "My father was an alcoholic. He was a weak man who was a pathological liar and an abusive drunk. Luckily, he died when I was sixteen. My mother had thirty-six years of him, though."

"Sorry."

"So I don't have a lot of patience with people like Paul Haig."

"Was Paul abusive to people?"

He frowned, then shrugged. "I guess not—not in the usual sense of 'abusive.' But he was totally spineless. He let his mother walk all over him and run his life. It sounded like she was a drunk too, and they were each other's enablers. A very sick situation. People like that don't kill themselves. They have better ways of escaping from reality. Better for them, anyway."

"You're the son of an alcoholic, Grey, but you drink. I take it that you can handle it."

"Yes, as a matter of fact I can handle it. I make it a point to."

"You talked, though, as if you thought there was something sinister about Paul's death. That it wasn't an accident."

"I wouldn't know for sure, of course. I didn't have anything specific in mind. And boozers can be awfully sloppy, so it could have been accidental. But there were people who hated Paul. That I do know. Though probably not enough to kill him, if that's what we're talking about here. That's going a little far."

I said, "Who do you have in mind?"

He drained his beer glass but made no move to order another.

78

"At least two of the guys in the therapy group hated his guts. And Paul talked in the group about other people he'd had serious run-ins with. Obviously his personality just got to some people."

"That can happen. Though rubbing somebody the wrong way rarely leads to homicide—except among urban schoolchildren these days, but that's another story. Who were the two guys in the group who hated Paul?"

"Roland Stover and Dean Moody. Have you talked to them yet?"

"No. They aren't a couple, are they? Isn't Moody the one who sued his parents for making him a homosexual?"

Oliveira grinned, apparently at the image of Stover and Moody as a couple. "Yeah, Dean's the wrathful son, but I doubt that he and Roland are dating. As far as I know, they both passed Crockwell 101 and have been certified het."

"What makes you say they hated Paul Haig?"

"They said so, in the group. They hated him for being wishy-washy about his sexuality, and for betraying the group by sucking Larry Bierly's dick and then leaving with him. Roland and Dean were the zealots in the group, the fanatical true believers."

"I heard one of them is a religious nut."

"Roland is. 'He who lieth with another man shall be put to death,' and all that. Dean was more of a secular humanist. He just thought homosexuality was sick."

"Did either Stover or Moody ever threaten Paul?"

He thought about this. "Not exactly," he said finally. "It was more of a general 'You'll pay for your evil, perverted ways, Paul.' More of a dire warning than an actual personal threat."

"I heard Crockwell once threatened Paul. Do you remember that?"

"It was just before Paul and Larry walked out last summer," Oliveira said. "It was truly shocking. It was a side of Crockwell we'd never seen before. He apologized later and tried to convince us it was a calculated outburst. But I think he was genuinely out of control. Something Paul or Larry said just got to Crockwell and he flipped out. Two of the guys were so shaken up by it, when I saw them outside after the session they talked about dropping out of the group."

"Which two said that?"

"Gary Moe and Nelson Bowkar. But you won't be interviewing them. They're dead."

"I heard."

"They both had AIDS and they went off the Patroon Bridge together. You want romance in your life? There's romance for you."

"Are you aware, Grey, of anyone ever making an audiotape of any of the therapy sessions with Crockwell?"

"No. Did somebody?"

"Possibly."

He glowered. "That's pretty shitty. What's on the tape? Have you heard it?"

"I can't discuss it, and I'm sure you understand why."

"Sure. It's confidential. But not so confidential that some cock-sucking private eye doesn't know all about it and is going around Albany asking questions about something in people's lives they had every right to expect would be kept totally private." The big gray eyes, sultry before, were cold now.

I said, "That's a more or less true assessment of what's happening. It's all in the service, though, of clearing up the circumstances surrounding Paul Haig's death, if that's any consolation. And of shedding light on the attempt on the life of Larry Bierly last night. Did you hear about that?"

"What? Somebody tried to kill Larry Bierly?"

"He was shot in the Millpond Mall parking lot. He's expected to survive."

"God, that's awful."

"Do you know a Steven St. James?"

"No. Should I?"

"Not necessarily."

"Who do they think shot Larry?"

"There are no suspects yet."

Oliveira said, "Ten guys started out last year in the therapy group we were in with Crockwell, and now three are dead and somebody tried to kill a fourth guy. You're cute, Strachey, and I'll bet you've got a nice one down there between those trim thighs. But for the kind of detective work that's needed on this case, I think they're going to have to bring in Oliver Stone."

That one was a little hard for me to sort out, but I salvaged from it what I thought I could before saying so-long-for-now to Grey Oliveira.

11

I arrived back at the house on Crow Street just as Timmy ambled around the corner after a hard day at the Assembly.

I said, "Think up some new ways to tax 'n' spend?"

"I tried, I tried."

We went inside and smooched behind closed doors, so as not to frighten the Morses, the elderly Presbyterians who lived in the townhouse next to ours and who often came out to polish the little Historical Albany Foundation plaque next to their front door. Our plaque was tarnished—fittingly Maude Morse had once told another neighbor.

"How is Larry Bierly doing?" Timmy asked, removing his jacket and placing it carefully on a wooden hanger he kept on the foyer hatrack specifically for this purpose. His necktie went over the banister by the newel post.

"He was improving, the last I heard. But I've got to check again with the hospital and the cops."

"Are you still conniving to ruin Vernon Crockwell?" Timmy's glistening shoes came off and were placed side by side on the far right of the fourth step.

"I'm still conniving to find out how and why Paul Haig died, and who shot Bierly and why. If Crockwell is mixed up in either situation, his evil mission will be destroyed. I'll be glad and so will you."

"What does 'mixed up in' mean? That's the part I'm nervous about." I followed him to the kitchen, where he fixed himself a tall, cool glass of Price Chopper seltzer. I found a Popsicle in the freezer.

"If it takes a load off your mind, Timothy, rest assured I don't plan on planting evidence in Crockwell's office—a smoking revolver or—in Paul Haig's case, what? That's the problem with Haig's death. Even if he was somehow forced or conned into ingesting the lethal combination of Scotch and Elavil, what evidence of it can anybody come up with at this late date? He's been dead and buried for two months. And Haig's apartment, where he died, has been cleaned out and rented to someone else. So physical evidence is going to be nil."

"That does leave you in the lurch. Who's your client? Got one yet?"

"I haven't decided. But the queue still winds around the block. That won't be a problem." He gave me his look that said, I'm not rolling my eyes theatrically but I would if I were the type who did that.

I said, "I'm talking to the members of the therapy group—I've met three so far—trying to get a clearer picture of the Crockwell-Haig-Bierly constellation and any potential violence in it, and how anybody else might have fit into it in a violent way. None of the three I talked to comes down especially hard on Crockwell—not as a murder or attempted-murder suspect anyway. Their opinion of him as a therapist is poor, but that's separate. Except, I heard the tape this morning that somebody sent to the cops, and Crockwell did threaten Haig. Each threatened the other, in fact. When Haig said he was quitting the group, Crockwell threatened to bring Phyllis Haig into it, and Haig said Crockwell would be sorry if he did, and Haig would stop him, and Crockwell said if Haig interfered Crockwell would stop him dead in his tracks."

" 'Dead in his tracks'? He used those words?"

"I heard it."

"Maybe the tape was edited to make it sound like he said that."

"No, I've got corroboration from three people who were there."

"Maybe they're the ones who edited the tape and sent it in."

"All three of them? That sounds overly conspiratorial for this particular situation."

"Maybe Mrs. Haig can shed some light on whether Crockwell contacted her and how Paul reacted."

"I plan on asking her," I said, "but shedding light is not her forte." I licked off the last of the Popsicle and placed the stick in the bin Timmy had set up by the sink labeled "Waste Wood Products." I knew where the paper, glass and plastic ended up, but I was never sure what he did with the wood.

I said, "Anyway, Crockwell is sounding more and more like a quack but less and less like a cold-blooded killer, and there are two members of the group I haven't met yet who sound much more problematical. I talked to two guys who survived Crockwell and are now a cozy couple themselves—sort of Fred Mertz married to Fred Mertz—and I met with a married man from Saratoga who is preoccupied with dick and who may be the most cynical man in North America. They're very different types, but all three of them mentioned two group members, Dean Moody and Roland Stover, who are violently antigay. They'll bear looking into."

Timmy said, "Gay homophobes. They're the worst."

"Maybe. The competition is keen. And then there's this: ever hear of a Steven St. James?"

"I don't think so. Any relation to Susan?"

"Not that I know of. I found him visiting Larry Bierly in the hospital this morning. He was cagey and evasive about his relationship with Bierly, and when I brought up Crockwell's group, he panicked and fled the premises. I went after him and pressed him on his connection to Bierly and Haig and Crockwell, and before he drove away, scared and shaken, he said, 'You don't want to know.'"

"Except you do. Who do you think he is?"

"No clue. I traced his car to Schuylers Landing. I'll track him down tomorrow."

"Maybe he's Bierly's boyfriend. Or he was Haig's or something. Or both. Or Crockwell's. Or—or all of theirs."

84

"I'd say your Irish Catholic imagination is running away with you on that one, Timothy."

"Yes, well, from the sounds of this curious and varied crew, your New Jersey Presbyterian imagination might not be up to the task."

"Funny, somebody else made a similar observation about an hour ago. Maybe I need to be open to more baroque explanations for whatever is going on here."

Timmy said, "Or even gothic."

I reached another of the therapy group by phone. Eugene Cebulka, in East Greenbush, agreed to meet me at seven-thirty at a Chinese restaurant we both knew out on Route 20.

I was about to call the hospital and Al Finnerty when the phone rang and Vernon T. Crockwell, sounding stricken, said, "I need your help quite badly, Donald. I'll pay you whatever your highest rate is. Just please do everything you can to find out who shot Larry Bierly—and killed Paul Haig if he was murdered and that's part of whatever this horrible thing is that's happening to me."

"To you, Vernon?"

"The police have questioned me again, and now they say they've found the gun that was used to shoot Larry Bierly. They say they found it in the dumpster behind my building!"

"Uh-oh."

"Can you imagine!"

"Yep."

"Someone is doing this to me!"

"That's what it looks like, Vernon."

"It's unjust. It's just terribly unjust. Now, Donald—Norris Jackacky tells me you are a fighter for justice."

"Me and the Green Hornet—and Al D'Amato too. Is he a hero of yours, Vernon?"

"Donald, are you going to help me or not? I must know! My wife must know! Doris is beside herself with fright and revulsion that this should be happening to our family, and the poor woman's near-hysteria is entirely justified."

I said, "I heard the tape."

"Oh. I see. So then you know that I never said anything illegal or unprofessional, strictly speaking."

"You threatened Haig. He threatened you and then you threatened to stop him dead in his tracks."

"I was speaking figuratively, as part of a therapeutic technique. I was merely trying to elicit a response. Although I do appreciate that the untrained lay observer might misunderstand."

"Vernon," I said, "you sure are full of it. You know, I'm starting to believe less and less of anything you tell me. I don't, for example, any longer consider plausible your reasons for trying to hire me. You say it's because I'm the best around. But I know and Norris Jackacky knows that there are other excellent investigators in Albany who are not homosexual, your particular bête noire. So please tell me the truth now. Why me?"

A long silence. I could hear him breathing hard. Then he said, "I'm ashamed to—what I mean to say is, I am simply unable to be as candid on some points as you might consider it appropriate for me to be. Let's just say, I have my reasons."

I said, "Are you gay yourself?"

"Of course not! That is perfectly absurd."

"Who is Steven St. James?" I said.

More shallow breathing. Then: "I have no idea. Steven who?"

"Vernon, for someone in your line of work, where sincerity— or at least the impression of sincerity—must count for a lot, you're a terrible liar." When this got no response except what sounded like a little mewing sound, I said, "I take it you have no alibi for last night when Bierly was shot, it being Thursday. Just like the night Paul Haig died."

"That's correct, unfortunately. No, I don't."

"One of three likely conclusions can be drawn from the fact, Vernon, that bad things happen to good people from one of your therapy groups on Thursday nights when you are, you say, alone in your office. One conclusion could be, it's a funny coincidence. A second, more interesting conclusion might be, you did it—

killed Paul Haig, shot Larry Bierly, and tossed the gun used to shoot Paul in the garbage bin behind your building."

"Oh, no. My Lord, how could I ever do such things! And how could I be so stupid that I'd throw the gun away in my own trash?"

"I don't know, Vernon. Psychology is your department. Maybe you were distraught and you panicked. Of course, a third obvious conclusion would be, somebody who knows your schedule is setting you up—committing a crime or crimes on Thursday night and then sending the letter and the tape to the police to implicate you, knowing you're alibiless, and throwing the gun in your dumpster for the police to find."

"Yes, yes, exactly. But who? Before he was shot, Donald, I thought it was probably Larry Bierly who was, as you term it, setting me up. But now it seems to be someone else entirely."

"Why did you think it was Bierly?"

"Well, Larry was—angry with me."

"Oh, that's a good reason."

"I mean," Crockwell said, "Larry was both so angry at himself for continuing treatment for as long as he did, and so angry at me for providing a therapy that he had lost faith in, that eventually he became totally consumed with hatred for me—unhinged, I must say, acting out uncontrollably."

"How do you know that? What did he say or do?"

Crockwell said nothing.

"Vernon?"

After a quarter-minute of labored breathing, he said, "Will you help me or won't you?"

"I don't know. I need to know more before I decide. What's the deal with you and Haig and Bierly? There's something you're not telling me."

No reply.

"You said that until yesterday you thought Bierly might be setting you up. Do you also think he killed Paul Haig?"

"I don't know."

"How does Steven St. James fit into this?"

"I don't know."

"Vernon, for a man on his knees begging for mercy, you're doing little of substance to gain my confidence."

"I'm offering you money," he whined, "and I'm not withholding any information that bears directly on the matter at hand. Can't you grasp that, Donald?"

"No, I can't. How do you know the information you're obviously withholding doesn't bear directly on the matter at hand? If you want me to work for you, I have to be the judge of that."

He let out a little moan of despair and hung up.

I sat for a minute waiting for the phone to ring again, but it didn't.

I called Al Finnerty at Division Two and caught him, he said, on the way out the door after a long but surprisingly productive day.

"Productive how?" I said.

"We think we've got the gun used to shoot Bierly, a mean little Raven MP-25, the weapon of choice for the playground criminals of America. Guess where we found it, Strachey?"

"In Crockwell's dumpster."

"You talked to Crockwell?"

"Just now. He's freaked, Al."

"So, Crockwell is your client? There's no harm done in getting that on the record. It won't change a thing, as far as I'm concerned. I'm just glad to know somebody's paying you a fat fee, Strachey."

"I'm not saying Crockwell is or isn't my client. I'm not saying the Infant of Prague is or isn't my client. I'm not saying because, for now, for a variety of reasons, I can't say. Do the ballistics check out on the gun?"

"Don't know yet. I can't get test results till Monday at the earliest."

"What about prints?"

"The same."

"But you're not charging Crockwell with anything?"

"Not just yet."

"How is Bierly doing?"

"Better. He's conscious. He wants to see you, Strachey."

"Good. I'll drop by. I take it he didn't ID who shot him."

"Nah. The shooter was crouched beside Bierly's car in the dark and fired across the roof of the car as Bierly was opening the door. Bierly thinks he was wearing a ski mask, but it happened so fast, he said, he wasn't even sure of that."

"That's not helpful."

"Bierly asked if we'd check on Vernon Crockwell's whereabouts last night. He said Crockwell ought to be our prime suspect. This was before we searched the dumpster. Bierly didn't know about the gun. Interesting, isn't it?"

"Yeah, interesting. Why did Bierly think it might have been Crockwell? Did he say?"

"He said Crockwell hated him for leaving his therapy group and taking Paul Haig with him. But that sounds weak to me."

"Me too, Al."

"Shrinks must have people coming and going and mad at them all the time. I've never heard of that leading to homicide."

"Me either."

"But Crockwell's still our best bet here. We've got the letter and the tape of him threatening Paul Haig, and he's got no alibi. Even if his prints aren't on the gun, if it's the one that shot Bierly, we'll probably have to charge him. I suppose all you gays will be delighted to hear that."

My grasp tightened on the receiver. I said, "That's not the strongest evidence to present to a jury, Al—a vague threat against a friend of Bierly's, the lack of an alibi, and a gun anybody could have tossed in Crockwell's dumpster. It's awfully circumstantial. Won't the DA need a little more?"

"Oh, we'll put it together," he said. "Especially if the ballistics check out. If Crockwell is your client, Strachey, I hope you got paid up front."

"I hope you're not being overly optimistic, Al." Or overly anything else.

"I want to close this out by the end of the month if I can. The worst that can happen is the DA will charge Crockwell, and because he's a professional type with no previous record he'll want to deal—plead to aggravated assault instead of attempted murder. And if he didn't do it, that'll come out in the wash too, and the case will be thrown out or he'll be acquitted. I've got a lot of faith in our system, Strachey. However it shakes out, we'll all have done our best, and that's what counts."

I said, "But even if Crockwell is innocent and sooner or later he's cleared, the chances are, once you shove him into the sausage machine he'll come out sausage, in the sense that he'll be ruined professionally."

"Well, I've heard the psychology field is overcrowded," Finnerty said, and I shuddered.

Before I left for my dinner appointment in East Greenbush, I gave Timmy a quick rundown of my conversations with Crockwell and Finnerty.

He said, "So what are you going to do?"

"I don't know."

"Some choices you've got. You can work for Crockwell, who's probably being sandbagged unfairly but who's a social menace who should be put out of business, though not for all the wrong reasons. You can go with Bierly, who's been victimized in all kinds of ways and deserves support, except he's apparently pathologically fixated on Crockwell in a way that clouds rather than clears the air. Or you can sign on with Phyllis Haig and use her money to get to the bottom of this thing, even though Larry Bierly probably didn't kill Paul, and she'd be paying you to prove that he did. Or, of course, you could just back away from the whole thing and let the Albany cops handle it in their inimitable fashion—with lives smashed to pieces in a random and whimsical way, law enforcement as theater of the absurd."

"That nicely sums up the hopelessly paradoxical nature of the situation, Timothy. Thank you."

"So which is it? Not to be overly pushy, but I guess now you have to go one way or the other."

"Not yet," I said. "I don't know enough yet. There's been so much evasiveness and dissimulation by all the parties in this whole affair that I'm sure there's a larger picture I'm not seeing and that's critical to my understanding the little I do know— about Paul Haig's death, and Larry Bierly's shooting, and Crockwell's fear and his odd attempts to hire me, of all people, and Phyllis Haig's attempts to blame her son's death on Bierly, and— Steven St. James. How is St. James connected to Bierly and Haig and, apparently, Crockwell? And what about Moody and Stover, the violent homophobes in the therapy group? There's just too much I need to know before I can be sure which way to head, and in whose employ."

"It sounds as if you should have a staff of fifty investigators working on this," Timmy said. "I hope it doesn't take you six months to sort it out."

"It could be time-consuming, I guess. But I'll take it one day at a time. I mustn't let myself become a slave to the temporal realm."

"True, true, but the mortgage is due on the first of June. Keep that in mind, will you?"

It was hell loving a man who got all his values from dead white European males, but to have done such was my complex destiny.

12

I saw no single men seated either at the bar or in the dining room of Would You Like to Take a Wok. But a male-female couple at a rear table seemed to be waiting for someone, and when they saw me peering quizzically, the man got up and came my way.

"Would you be looking for Gene Cebulka?"

"Yes, I'm Don Strachey."

"Glad to meet you. I brought my wife along. I hope that's okay."

"Sure, that's up to you."

He was a well-scrubbed, ruddy-faced man in his late twenties in crisply laundered khakis and a pale pink polo shirt that matched the restaurant linen. He had a broad grin and a country-boy lope, and he could have passed for a soda-fountain boy on a *Saturday Evening Post* cover from 1952 had it not been for his ravaged head. Cebulka's honey-colored hair was thick in spots but in others it was missing altogether. This was a result not of disease, it soon became apparent, but of Cebulka's habit of absently tugging at clumps of his hair as he spoke. This seemingly pleasant young man with a look and demeanor as wholesome as any I'd run into in recent decades was, clump by clump, pulling his hair out by the roots.

"And this is my wife, Tracy," Cebulka said, smiling, as he twisted and tugged at his head. "Tracy, this is Mr. Strachey."

"Don. Nice to meet you, Tracy."

She was freckled and pretty and slight under a mainsail of

permed hair broad enough to launch a brigantine. She looked scared to death of me, but squeaked out, "Hi."

"Tracy thought if I was going to meet a good-looking man in a restaurant, she better come along and keep an eye on me," Cebulka joked, but Tracy just looked embarrassed. I probably did too.

Then it was my turn to put my foot in it. "So, how long have you honeymooners been married? Six months? Six weeks?"

"Eleven years," Tracy said sadly.

"Oh. So—you were already married then, Gene, when you went into Vernon Crockwell's program. I'd have guessed you were younger."

"I'm twenty-eight," he said, "and Tracy's twenty-seven."

"Ah."

"I just figured," Cebulka said brightly, "that I better get my ducks in a row before Tracy and I started a family. If you catch my meaning." He winked.

I was about to come up blank but was saved by the waiter, who arrived with red-tassled menus the size of the gates to Nanking. The three of us set about studying these and after a time summoned the waiter and placed our order for an assortment of multicolored edibles in cornstarch. Tracy Cebulka glanced at me nervously, and Gene smiled and twisted his hair.

When the waiter was gone, I said, "Gene, I guess your experience with Vernon Crockwell's program was a happy one. And it achieved the outcome you desired."

"That's true," he said, his fingers busy above. "I used to be turned on by men, but that was strictly no-win. I had a chance to be straightened out, so to speak, and I availed myself of the opportunity. Fortunately, Dr. Crockwell's way did the trick."

"Now Gene plays softball with the guys," Tracy said.

This was followed by another silence. After a moment, I said, "It's hard to argue with success."

They both looked at me, Tracy unmoving, Gene twisting away at a recalcitrant clump.

"Although," I said, "Crockwell's therapy apparently doesn't do

93

the trick for everybody. Paul Haig and Larry Bierly, for instance. Their departure from the group was a bitter one, I'm told."

"I saw on the news Larry was in a shooting," Cebulka said. "I hope he's going to pull through. That's a terrible tragedy after Paul passing away and all."

I said it looked as if Bierly was going to be okay.

"I'm glad," Cebulka said. "Larry's sincere in his beliefs. I guess he turned into a kind of gay libber, didn't he?"

"Kind of."

"I'm broad-minded. If that's what makes a person happy, I say, hey, go for it. But going with guys never made me happy. It just made me feel guilty as heck."

"Gene used to come home late at night from Albany and just sit out on the porch feeling like a total asshole," Tracy said. "Even if it was ten below."

"Now I never go to Albany at all anymore," Cebulka said. "I don't need to. I haven't set foot in the place for—it'll be seven months next Wednesday."

"He's turned into a real stay-at-home," Tracy said. "Which I happen to like."

"A real couch potato," Cebulka said with a laugh.

"Of course, it would be nice if he got off the couch once in a while too," Tracy said, her hopeful look fading. "Especially like not falling asleep downstairs every single solitary night of the week."

"I'm hooked on Jay Leno," Cebulka said with a sheepish grin. "What can I tell you? Jay just cracks me up."

More silence. Then I said, "But tell me, Gene. Back when you were still in the group, I've gotten the impression that things didn't always go so smoothly for everybody. That there was a certain amount of tension and conflict."

"Well, naturally there was going to be," Cebulka said. "Here we were, dealing with a lot of heavy-duty stuff from our formative years. Deformative years, in our cases. Since homosexuals don't bond with their fathers normatively, they have to learn later on how to bond with other men in a normal way. That's what we

94

were trying to do all the time, and it was no Sunday-school picnic, believe you me. It was hard work, and we were all working a double shift—getting rid of our old habits of trying to get into guys' pants and practicing at the same time how to be a buddy and a pal and—you know—getting in touch with our true guyness. People would blow off steam sometimes, which is understandable. Once the toothpaste is out of the tube, it can be a dickens of a time getting it back in."

They both looked at me. Cebulka had a tight grip on a knot of hair and was working it loose.

I said, "Gene, when you heard about Paul Haig's suicide, did it surprise you?"

"No," he said without hesitation. "I was sad to hear it, but it didn't really surprise me."

"Why not?"

"Because I think what Paul really wanted in life was the love of a good woman. And when he quit Dr. Crockwell's treatment program, he probably figured he was dipped, as far as a woman."

"Do you have a particular woman in mind?"

"What? You mean besides Tracy?"

"I mean for Paul."

"Oh, I don't know who it would be. That would be up to Paul. But Larry was—I think he could keep being a homosexual and it wouldn't bother him. He sure was one tough nut to crack for Dr. Crockwell. Poor ol' Crocky. But I think Paul could have been saved if Larry hadn't led him down the garden path. Paul didn't have the willpower to resist temptation, though, and I guess he was so ashamed, he could no longer go on living. And I can relate to that. Paul has my deepest sympathy. Without Dr. Crockwell's help and Tracy's supportiveness, there but for the grace of God go I, possibly."

Tracy placed her hand on Cebulka's free one and gave it a squeeze.

I said, "Some people think that Paul's suicide wasn't any such thing, but that he was murdered."

"Whoa."

"And that someone in the group or connected to the group in some way is the killer."

"Holy Jehelka!"

"Ever hear of a Steven St. James?"

"No. Who's that?"

"I'm not sure yet. Gene, did anyone in the group ever threaten anyone else in the group or show signs of becoming violent?"

He screwed up his face. Tracy was big-eyed. Cebulka said, "When you called me up earlier, and you said you wanted to talk about Paul's suicide and Dr. Crockwell's program, I figured you were with Dr. Crockwell's insurance company or what have you, maybe some type of malpractice lawsuit, and I could put in a good word for the doc—happy to help him out after all the help he gave me. But now you're telling me somebody thinks somebody murdered Paul? Where in the world did a crazy idea like that get started?"

The waiter approached and set plates of two egg rolls each in front of Gene and Tracy and a bowl of hot-and-sour soup in front of me. When he was gone, I said, "There is some circumstantial evidence pointing to Dr. Crockwell's involvement—in Larry Bierly's shooting and maybe even Paul Haig's death. It's possible he'll be charged."

Cebulka stared at me and momentarily ceased his labors above. Tracy said, "But Dr. Crockwell has done so much good for people. How can they do this to him?"

"Who else in the group might have wanted to hurt Paul?" I asked. "Or shoot Larry Bierly? It's not clear yet, but the two events might be connected."

Tracy perked up. "Tell him," she said, "about—what's-their-names? Those two guys."

Cebulka was twisting away again with one hand, attempting with the other to cut a hunk off the end of an egg roll, which appeared to have been manufactured from a shingle-like material.

"You mean Dean and Roland?" Gene said.

"Yeah."

He abandoned the egg roll. Tracy ignored hers. I sipped at my smooth soup.

Cebulka said, "There were two guys in the group named Roland Stover and Dean Moody. They were always pretty down on gays—very negative, if you know what I mean. Gays are sinners, et cetera. They always talked like that in the group. Then when the group ended last December, I thought, one good thing is, I'll never have to listen to their hot air again. But then, lo and behold, I ran into them—about a month ago, I think. Over at Pizza Hut. Tracy was even with me. I introduced her to those two bozos. Jeez."

I said, "They were together?"

"Yeah, their table was right near our booth. Dean had salad bar and Roland was eating off of it too, and I'll bet Dean went back three times if he went back once. I think it says right on a sign, no sharing. The waitress saw it too, but she never let on."

"And you spoke to them?"

"For a minute."

"What did they have to say?"

Cebulka shook his head, a complicated maneuver. "Roland said, did I hear about Paul Haig? And I said yes, wasn't that too bad. And then do you know what Roland said?"

"No."

"He said, 'Paul had it coming.' "

"That's all?"

"No. He said, 'He who lieth with another man shall be put to death.' And then Dean said, 'Larry should die too,' and something about if American civilization is going to survive, it has to purge itself of people like that."

I said, "But this condemnation didn't include you—or themselves, of course."

"No, why should it? We all had our certificates by that time."

"You were certified heterosexual?"

97

Cebulka nodded vigorously, and a good-sized clump of hair came out in his hand. We all looked at it.

After a moment Tracy said, "Gene has a scalp condition."

Cebulka shrugged. "I guess it runs in the family. I have an uncle with the same condition."

13

I parted company with the Cebulkas around nine and headed back into Albany. I told them I might need to be in touch again and they said fine. Gene said next time I should bring the wife along. I let it go.

Following the revelation about Moody and Stover, not previously known to be a pair, I'd asked Cebulka about the session where Bierly and Haig had walked out of therapy amid a crossfire of recriminations. But Cebulka remembered the event only hazily and said Crockwell's outburst, while unusual, didn't have any lasting effects. After Haig and Bierly left, the group just picked up and proceeded without them.

Visiting hours at Albany Med were over, so I'd have to wait until morning to talk to Larry Bierly. I went home and called my machine. Nothing from Crockwell or Finnerty, but Phyllis Haig had left a minute's worth of breathy pauses and slurred imprecations.

While Timmy read a travel book called *Around the World by Yak and Kayak,* by Maynard Sudbury, one of the Peace Corps old boys Timmy knew from his long-ago but fondly remembered days in Andhra Pradesh, I tried to reach Roland Stover and Dean Moody, the only two surviving members of the therapy group I hadn't met yet.

I got no answer at the number I had for Moody, but just as I was about to hang up, a man breathing hard picked up the phone at Roland Stover's residence.

"Yes?"

"Is this Roland Stover?"

"Yes, and who is this?" He sounded tense and mean, fitting the consensus description I had.

"Hi, Roland, I'm Don Strachey, an investigator doing some work that might be of assistance to Dr. Vernon Crockwell. Dr. Crockwell didn't give me your name, but it was provided by another member of the psychotherapy group you were in. Could we get together some time soon so that I could ask you a couple of questions about the group? Dr. Crockwell might be having some legal problems, and there's a chance you could shed some light on the situation."

"What kind of legal problems?" Stover growled. "What do you mean by that?"

"Well, if we could sit down over a cup of coffee—"

"And who has the right to give you my name? That is a breach of medical confidentiality, and I demand to know this minute who gave you my name!"

"Larry Bierly did. He thought if I talked to you, Roland, I might come away with some insights into Dr. Crockwell's therapy group and who his friends and enemies in it are."

"I can tell you right now," Stover snapped, "that I am Vernon Crockwell's friend and Larry Bierly is his number-one enemy. Anyway, I heard on TV that somebody shot Larry, so how did you get my name from him?"

"He gave it to me before he was shot."

"Is he dead?"

"No. It looks as though he'll recover."

"Too bad. Sorry to hear it. Did you know Larry was an unrepentant sexual deviant?"

"I'm aware that he did not successfully complete Vernon Crockwell's course of therapy. But you did, I understand."

"Yes, I did. Dr. Crockwell along with the Holy Scriptures saved me from a life of moral corruption."

"I'd like to hear about that, and whatever additional information you'd be willing to share about Dr. Crockwell's mission. Could we meet somewhere?"

100

A pause. "Did you say you're a private investigator?"

"Yes, I am."

"Who is employing you?"

"I'm sorry, but I can't divulge that. My client must remain anonymous for now. I can tell you, however, that in this matter and many others I have a strong interest in moral truth." I was looking across the room at Timmy, whose eyes came up from his book.

"Well, what exactly are you investigating?" Stover said. "Deviancy?"

"That might play a part in it. Incidentally, there's another member of the Crockwell therapy group I haven't been able to get hold of. Are you in touch with Dean Moody, by chance?"

"Yes, I'm in touch with Dean."

"Perhaps we could all get together and I could pick your brains—I mean yours and Dean's—about deviancy. For this investigative study I'm doing." Timmy placed his book in his lap and watched me.

"Well, then, what about tomorrow after work?" Stover said. "I'm a sales associate at Wal-Mart on Route 4, and I get home around five-thirty." He gave me his Albany address.

"I'd be pleased to drop by then," I said. "I hope Dean can make it too."

"I'll have to check with him," Stover said, and hung up.

Timmy said, "Wasn't that a little misleading?"

"Yep."

"Which one were you talking to?"

I said it was Roland Stover, and I described Stover and Dean Moody and their feverish homophobia and their apparent status as a twosome of some sort.

"Do you think maybe they killed Paul Haig?"

"No, probably not."

"Or shot Larry Bierly?"

"Maybe, but I doubt it. It's possible they did one or the other, or both crimes, assuming Paul Haig's death was even a crime, which hasn't been established. But so far I'd have to say I doubt either Stover or Moody was involved in either event. They both sound hateful and deranged enough to hurt people badly, maybe even physically. But so far there's no real connection I've heard about between either of them and Paul and Larry, except for two things: in the group they had hissy fits over Paul's and Larry's gay-and-proud departure, and of course there's their glee over the death and misfortune of the two brazen sodomites. But they don't act guilty of actual murder or assault. They're completely open and unashamed about their hatreds, and they're probably no more than a couple of obnoxious gasbags. People like that can be psychopathic killers—I know, it wouldn't be unprecedented—and I'm going to stay alert and open to the possibility. But what I'm really after now is a clearer picture of Crockwell, Paul Haig, Phyllis Haig, and Larry Bierly and some weird dynamic among them that none of them has been forthcoming about. I think that's where the key lies to Paul Haig's death—whether it was murder or suicide—and maybe to Larry Bierly's getting shot. And it seems this Steven St. James—Mr. You-Don't-Want-to-Know—fits in somewhere too. Though as to where, beats me."

"So tomorrow you're meeting this Stover thug posing as an investigator on deviancy?"

"Something like that."

"I could come along and vouch for your interest in the subject."

"Right, and my expertise."

"If he asked about your scholarship, I could say, 'His life is his treatise.' "

"You don't really want to come along, do you? This is all in jest."

"No," he said, "I don't want to get anywhere near Stover or Moody. They may not be as interesting and mysterious and murky in their motives as Crockwell and Bierly and the Haigs and this other guy, but they do sound truly dangerous."

"Maybe you're right. I'm not sure what to think. Bierly is conscious now. I'll talk to him tomorrow. That might help."

"Maybe he'll shed some light."

"Yes," I said, "if shedding light is anything he really wants to come out of all this. Nailing Crockwell at any cost seems to be his main aim. Nobody really seems to want to shed light, and I've got to find out why."

14

Saturday morning at ten, before heading over to Albany Med, I phoned Phyllis Haig.

"Well," she said, "you're goddamned hard to get ahold of. I've been trying to reach you for days. I'd've had better luck trying to get a rise out of Dick Tracy than getting one out of you. So, Don, what's your pleasure? Are you gonna rob me blind and go to work for me and put that little fairy Larry Bierly behind bars where he belongs, or am I going to have to go out and find a real man for the job? Say, I see somebody shot Bierly and put him in the hospital. Too bad. I'd much rather see justice take its course. It wasn't you that shot him, was it? Jay Tarbell never said you were a hit man, which wasn't exactly what I had in mind. Though you call a lawyer these days and you never know what kind of stunt they're going to pull, just so they can charge you top dollar for it."

I didn't think she'd started drinking yet—my guess was she observed the proprieties of her class by holding off until 12:05—but otherwise she was in vintage form.

I said, "No, Phyllis, I didn't shoot Larry Bierly. Did you?"

"No, I didn't, Don. I didn't drive out to Millpond at midnight the other night brandishing my forty-four and plug Bierly in the gut. At least, not as far as I can recall, I didn't. So if I didn't do it, and you didn't do it, what was it, a mugging?"

"It doesn't appear to have been. Nothing was taken."

"The little homo probably staged the whole thing. Everybody knows what a conniver he is."

I said, "Why would he do that, Phyllis?"

"Well, how the hell should I know? You're the one who's supposed to be . . . Now look. I've done everything but hire a detective to get ahold of the detective—that's Y-O-U—who was supposed to let me know two days ago if you're gonna help me out on this goddamn thing or not. So, Mr. Hard-to-Get-Ahold-Of Strachey, what is the verdict?"

I said, "Sorry to have been out of touch, Phyllis, but I've been doing some preliminary snooping around before I decide whether or not to take your money. I'll let you know one way or another in a day or so for sure if I'm going to hire on with you. But first I've got some questions that need answering, and there are a couple of them that you can answer."

"Oh, really? What questions? I hope this isn't going to be some kind of third degree. Larry Bierly is the one you should be grilling, not me. So, what do you want to ask me?"

I said, "After Larry and Paul left Crockwell's therapy group, did Crockwell ever contact you?"

After a little silence, she said, "I don't know what that has to do with the price of tea in China."

"Before he was shot, I spoke with Larry Bierly, who said when he and Paul left the therapy group, Crockwell threatened to turn you against Paul unless Paul reconsidered and continued therapy. My question is, did Crockwell ever try to do that?"

Another pause. "Well, I don't remember exactly what Dr. Crockwell had to say to me at that point in time. I suppose we must have chatted."

"Uh-huh."

"I know I asked for my money back—I'd paid him a goddamned small fortune—and never got so much as a red cent out of that chiseler."

"When Dr. Crockwell spoke with you, was he critical of Paul?"

"He was none too pleased with the outcome, if that's what you mean."

"But who did he blame it on?"

"Crockwell accepted no responsibility for himself, I can tell you that, Mr. Don, private eye. That would have left him open for a lawsuit, and for all he knew I could have been taping the conversation. Doctors don't pass gas anymore without checking with their lawyers first."

I said, "Have you secretly taped conversations in the past?"

"No, why on earth are you asking me that?"

"You said Crockwell might have suspected that you were."

"God, I can't even get my friggin' VCR to work."

"Did Paul ever record people's conversations that you know of?"

"No. Now what are you getting at? Does somebody have something on tape?"

"The Albany police were sent a recording of the therapy session that Paul and Bierly walked out of and never came back. The sender remains anonymous. Accompanying the tape was a note implicating not Larry Bierly but Vernon Crockwell in Paul's death. There's no proof, just the tape, on which Crockwell says a lot of nasty stuff about Paul's sexuality and threatens to come between you and Paul if Paul quits therapy. When Paul warns Crockwell not to interfere in his family life and says he won't allow Crockwell to mess things up between you and Paul, Crockwell proclaims that he will not be impeded in his noble work, and he tells Paul that if he gets in the way Crockwell will stop him dead in his tracks. Those are Crockwell's words: 'I'll stop you dead in your tracks.' Are you familiar with any of this, Phyllis?"

A silence.

"Moreover," I went on, "on Wednesday you told me that Larry Bierly had threatened Crockwell, and Crockwell had it on tape. But it wasn't Crockwell who sent the cops the tape, and it wasn't Bierly who was recorded threatening Crockwell. It was Paul."

She did not reply, and after a moment I became aware that Mrs. Haig was quietly weeping.

"Are you there, Phyllis? Are you okay?"

She sniffled and said, in a breaking voice, "I don't know who taped what. I just know what Paul told me. Oh, poor, poor Paul. I want Paul. I want my son back. I want my Paul."

"What happened is terrible for you, Phyllis. It's bad, I know."

Choking back tears, she said, "Paul didn't kill himself, did he? Am I right? I was—maybe I said the wrong things. Yes, I know I did, I know maybe I did. But Paul wouldn't kill himself over that. Paul was used to me." She snuffled and blew her nose next to the phone.

I said, "Phyllis, the police actually have some good evidence now showing that Paul could not have killed himself. And as for you and Paul—hey, it's clear from the tape, which I've heard, that you and Paul hit it off, and he was used to you and devoted to you."

"I know I said some things that were harsh. But it was all tough love, you know? Am I right?"

"I know what you're saying."

"I even got Paul another doctor. To help Paul—goddamn get on with it. Whatever."

I said, "What doctor was this?"

"Glen Snyder in Ballston Spa. Deedee went to him for a while after her marriage broke up. He's not—I mean, he's just a regular head shrinker. Pills and whatnot. I was even going to foot the bill, but Paul only went five times before he died, so it only ended up costing me seven-fifty. So I was trying to do it Paul's way, wasn't I? Even if I opened my big yap once too often, maybe, right after Paul left Dr. Crockwell, later on I made it up to him by doing it his way. Am I right?"

"It sounds as if you were doing your best, Phyllis. Was it Dr. Snyder who prescribed the Elavil?"

"Yeah. And ain't that a kick in the head? It looks like indirectly I'm the one who supplied that treacherous homicidal maniac Larry Bierly with the murder weapon."

Back to that again. I said, "Larry Bierly tells a different story about Paul's finances from the one you told me. You said you thought Larry killed Paul for his lucrative business. Larry claims Beautiful Thingies is deeply in debt and, for the foreseeable future, more of a burden than a help. He said Paul was swindled by an assistant manager during a period when Paul was drinking too much to notice and he nearly lost the business late last year."

"That is a lie!"

"It will be easy for me to check."

"Then do it, do it."

"And I'm sorry to have to remind you, Phyllis, that serious financial problems sometimes trigger suicide in people who are shaky otherwise. Isn't it possible that—"

She had begun to sob.

"Phyllis?"

Then a crash and a dial tone.

Now what had I said? I thought I'd described a possible suicide motive—financial desperation—that took Mrs. Haig more or less off the hook even if the murder theory somehow didn't pan out. But instead, something I said had pushed her over the edge. It was something I kept doing to people as I stumbled around in the darkness, and that darkness was one that the people I was hurting were choosing not to illuminate. Why?

15

Y ou were right about one thing," I told Bierly. "It does look as if Paul did not commit suicide." I told him about the pill canister lid that could not have been put back on and tightened by someone who was already drunk.

"Oh, so I was right about one thing? Then what are the things I was wrong about?"

He had a big gauze packing taped to the side of his neck and a bulky wad of something under his hospital nightie that was covering up the chest wound. Luckily, he'd just told me, the neck injury was superficial, missing the carotid by a quarter of an inch, and the chest wound wasn't as serious as it could have been: a bullet had ricocheted off the car door, à la Ronald Reagan, and entered Bierly's left chest, shattering two ribs but missing vital organs. His recovery, his doctors had told him, would be slow but total.

"One thing you were wrong about," I said, "was your account of your and Paul's exit from Crockwell's therapy group. You told me Crockwell blew up and threatened you and threatened Paul—which he did. But what you didn't tell me was, Crockwell's threat was in response to Paul's vow to use any means to stop Crockwell from coming between Paul and his mother."

He gazed at me, red-eyed and sallow, but said nothing. He was propped up, his arms limp at his sides, an IV drip tube stuck in his thick right forearm. Even in repose Bierly's body looked powerful, and I was reminded anew of the destructive force of a metal projectile shot from a cheap mechanism that any deranged twerp could pick up on a street corner.

Finally, he said, "How do you know what was said that day? Were you there? I don't remember seeing you there, Strachey."

"I've heard a tape of the session," I said.

Bierly squinted at me perplexedly. Then he suddenly croaked out, "That slimeball!"

"What slimeball?"

"Crockwell. Who else would have taped the session?"

"You're missing a point, Larry, that happens to be your own. The point is, whatever you said, or Paul said, at that session, it's Crockwell who comes off worst. He said if Paul interfered with him, he'd stop Paul dead in his tracks. Do you remember that?"

"I guess so," he said weakly, not looking me in the eye. What was with Bierly? He wanted more than anything, he kept telling me, to nail the wicked Crockwell, while at the same time there was a part of him that didn't want to have to confront Crockwell or even discuss him in any detail. Bierly loathed Crockwell, but for reasons I had yet to decipher he was afraid of him too, or at least reluctant to provoke him.

I said, "It wasn't Crockwell who made a tape. It must have been a member of the group. Somebody sent the tape to the cops anonymously with a note suggesting Crockwell murdered Paul. The implication was, Paul had somehow gone after Crockwell for trying to poison Paul's relationship with his mother and Crockwell killed him. That sounds farfetched to me—Crockwell has no history of violence—just as it sounded unlikely when you told me you thought Crockwell killed Paul just because Crockwell was a hater obsessed with homosexuality. I've met the guy, and he is that. But he seems to get his rocks off taking gay men's money and torturing them with his treatments. He doesn't need to be homicidal. Of course, the cops like the looks of him because he's got a sort of motive for shooting you and maybe killing Paul, and he's got no alibi for either. I know, Larry, that you didn't shoot yourself twice, but I'm wondering if it was you who made

110

the tape and sent it to the cops to set Crockwell up as a suspect in Paul's death. Was it?"

He'd been watching me and listening with effort—he was undoubtedly on heavy-duty painkillers—and after a moment he said simply, "No. I didn't even know a tape existed."

"Who might have recorded it?"

He shook his head. "Who knows. Everybody in that group was weird or fucked up in some way. And I always had a feeling they all had their secrets. I know some of them did. I'd see Gary Moe and Nelson Bowkar together at the mall sometimes, and once I saw LeVon Monroe and Walter Tidlow eating together late at night at the Denny's on Wolf Road. It came out later that Gary and Nelson were lovers, and it wouldn't surprise me if LeVon and Walter were getting it on too. Paul told me he even saw one of the group cruising a tearoom one time. Maybe somebody taped all the sessions and went home and played them back and jerked off. It's not your well-adjusted healthy homosexual who's drawn into a lunatic asylum like Crockwell's."

"Who did Paul catch in a tearoom?"

"He never said. This happened sometime last winter, I think. But it's hazy because Paul never brought it up again. He went in to take a piss somewhere, he said, and there was some wild scene going on. This guy was in the thick of it. He was telling me this on the phone—saying guess who he saw violating both the canons of good taste and his therapy contract with Crockwell—when his call waiting went off and it was Phyllis, so that was that. Phyllis always took precedence with Paul. The next time I saw him, I asked him about the tearoom scene, but he didn't seem to want to talk about it. I got the idea that maybe his presence in this place wasn't entirely innocent either."

"You claim to value being honest and straightforward, Larry. And yet there is another area where you have not been entirely honest and straightforward with me."

"Oh, is that so?" He looked wary.

"You forgot or chose not to explain to me the connection

between you and Paul and Crockwell and Steven St. James. You can correct that oversight starting as soon as I count to one. One."

Bierly was hooked up to some kind of electric monitor, and as he lay there looking over at me, a couple of his numbers started going up.

For a second time, I said, "One."

Then he shook his head and said, "That has nothing to do with anything."

"I don't believe it."

"So don't."

"Who is St. James?"

"An acquaintance."

"More than that, I think. He was here first thing yesterday morning. He drove up from Schuylers Landing as soon as he heard on the news that you had been shot. Who is he, Larry?"

Bierly shifted irritably and gave me a get-off-my-back look. "Damn it, he's just a friend. Why are you making such a big fucking deal out of Steven? You're going on and on about unimportant crap like that and you're not doing your job at all, which is to nail that psychotic madman Crockwell. You said you believe me now that Paul didn't kill himself. So does this mean that you are working for me and not that ridiculous old bag Phyllis Haig?"

I said, "I'm pretty much convinced that Paul was murdered, and privately the cops are convinced too—though getting the DA to act may take some doing, inasmuch as the coroner has ruled that Paul died by his own hand, and when an old boy of official Albany is apprised of the incompetence of another old boy of official Albany, he tends not to shout it from the tallest tree. But be assured I'm working on all that. As for working for you— maybe. I do want to avoid taking your money if there's a good chance I can take the money from somebody else who has more than you do and deserves it less."

"Jesus, Strachey, you wouldn't last in business more than a week."

That hurt, though at least T. Callahan was not present for this affirmation of his own harsh view on the subject. I said, "So did

112

Crockwell shoot you? The cops said you were not able to identify who shot you."

Looking grave, he said, "I don't know exactly. I mean, it must have been Crockwell. Who else could it be? It all happened so fast—it's just blurry. The guy was wearing a ski mask, I think. He just rose up from the other side of the car, and the next thing I remember is, I was in the hospital. Did the cops question Crockwell? Are they going to arrest him? I didn't get a good look, but, God, it must have been him."

"They're talking to him. It's possible he'll be charged. There is some circumstantial evidence—a gun like the one used to shoot you has been found in Crockwell's office dumpster."

Bierly's eyes got big, and he said, "Christ!"

"Even if Crockwell's fingerprints aren't on the gun, Finnerty and his gang will probably pop Crockwell in their microwave and see if his ions start rearranging themselves. They're efficient down there on Arch Street."

Now Bierly looked truly frightened. "Is Crockwell being watched? I know the hospital has a guard outside my door, but Crockwell is ruthless. And if it was him, he could probably talk his way in here and come after me again."

"The cops may or may not have him under surveillance, but I was questioned and frisked before the guard let me in here, and I'd say not to worry. So, what is it that I don't want to know?"

"What?"

"Yesterday, Steven St. James got all spooked when I asked him questions about his connection to you and Paul and Vernon Crockwell. And before he went off in a tizzy, he said to me— when I asked him how you all were mixed up together—'You don't want to know.' Those were his words. 'You don't want to know.' My question to you, Larry, is, Why don't I?"

He stared at me hard, and he blushed. He had a forty-eight–hour growth of heavy black beard, and his color from the trauma and drugs and shock and exhaustion was a kind of baby-shit yellow, and yet through all that it was plain that Bierly was blushing—as he had three days earlier in the pizza parlor when I'd brought up Phyllis Haig's accusation that he had threatened Crockwell with violence and Crockwell had it on tape.

Bierly said, "Look, it really doesn't have anything to do with anything, but Steven is somebody I was mixed up with for a while during the winter, after Paul and I split up. The relationship never went anywhere serious."

"What's Crockwell got to do with it?"

He stared at me. "Nothing."

"Not according to Steven."

"Oh, really? What did he say?"

"That I don't want to know what you and Paul and Steven were involved in together. But I do want to know. In fact, Larry, if I'm going to consider working for you at all, I'll have to insist on knowing. I'm sure you can understand why I need to avoid groping around in the dark."

Bierly shut his eyes tight and said nothing. The silence lengthened and I let it. He was thinking hard about something, and his numbers were dancing around wackily again. When after a minute or two he opened his eyes, he looked at me exhaustedly and he said, "I've changed my mind."

"Uh-huh."

"I mean about hiring you."

"Oh?"

"It's really better if you leave this whole situation alone, Strachey. The cops will find out who shot me—and as for Paul, he's dead, so what difference does anything make? It sounds like the cops are going to drag Crockwell through the slime, he'll be ruined. And that's all I care about. So I think you'd just better skip it. Okay?" His medical condition—or something—seemed to overtake him and his eyes fluttered shut.

I said, "What made you change your mind so suddenly?"

Bierly didn't open his eyes, but his face tightened and he said, "I'm too tired for this."

"You'll regain your strength."

"That's my decision. You better go, Strachey. Please. Just go. Please."

114

"If you say so."

"Thanks for your help."

I said, "I may sign on with Phyllis, or even Crockwell if I think he's innocent and he's being railroaded. So I may see you soon again, Larry."

"No, please don't. I want you to let me alone."

"For now, sure."

"No, this isn't working. Please don't come back. You have to go now. Right now. Go." His eyes opened and they were full of pain.

"Okay. That's plain enough. So long, Larry."

He turned away.

I went out, nodded to the security guard, made my way down to the main floor and outside onto New Scotland Avenue, where the lilacs, some of which weren't lilac at all but creamy white, swayed heavily in the breeze. Why were creamy white lilacs still called lilacs? Why weren't they called creamy whites? Of course, not all roses were rose. Or grapes grape. Or petunias petunia.

I'd done it again. What had I said?

Back on Crow Street, I phoned my machine, on which two messages had been left. Vernon Crockwell's said, "I will not be needing your services after all. I have retained other professional help. Please do not contact me." Phyllis Haig's said, "I never want to speak to you again. You're fired!"

Timmy came downstairs and said, "What's up? Any news? Have you decided who you're going to work for?"

I said, "I'm thinking of a career change. Can you think of any other work I might be suited for?"

He said no.

16

D on't be despondent," Timmy said. "It's ten days till the first of the month. You'll get work And if you don't—so, you'll dip into capital."

"That's not funny." He knew that my "capital" consisted mainly of the six-year-old Mitsubishi I was driving south from Albany down the thruway, Timmy next to me in the tattered front passenger seat. "Anyway, I've got several accounts due. Chances are, somebody will pay me before June first."

"You mean like Alston Appleton?"

"I guess I'd better not count on that one." Appleton was a local venture capitalist whose operations were murky. I'd spent a month successfully tracking down his ex-wife and her coke-addict mother after they'd made off with a safe-deposit box full of Appleton's cash, only to present my bill for $7,100 to Appleton on the morning of the March day the SEC caught up with him and froze his assets. I was informed a month later by an ostentatiously unsympathetic federal official that with luck I might collect three or four cents on the dollar some time in the first quarter of the next century.

"Tell me again," Timmy said, "why Phyllis Haig got mad at you."

"I don't think I know. I thought I was allaying what I perceived to be her guilt over the way she had treated Paul, and over his possible suicide, by connecting his death to his financial problems, which she in no way had caused. Not that she was actually guiltless in Paul's troubles—far from it. But in that one respect, finances, she wasn't guilty, as far as I know. So I was trying to take some of the onus off her."

"Maybe," Timmy said, "Paul went to his mother for money when he was desperate and she turned him down."

"Mmm."

"So when you told her that financial pressure might have triggered Paul's suicide, or his getting himself murdered, it reminded her of her secret fear: that if she had bailed him out when his assistant manager absconded, he might be alive today. You made her rationalization crumble too—that Larry Bierly had actually killed Paul somehow. In your Chekhovian manner, you destroyed Mrs. Haig's illusions, and she sank into the doldrums and banished you from her estate."

"The literary reference sounds inapt—try Inge, or maybe Bram Stoker. But otherwise what you say sounds plausible."

"That's what it sounds like to me," Timmy said.

We sped past the exit for Saugerties, where plans were under way for a big Woodstock reunion concert. That peculiar era was long gone, and I doubted more than a handful of people would show up.

I said, "I believe now that Paul Haig was murdered, but maybe Phyllis no longer really believes it—thanks to me—and that's why she can't stand the thought of me. Why didn't I think of that?"

"Because you're understandably confused. Everybody in this thing seems to be carrying some guilty secret around that's connected to Paul Haig's death—or at least they think it's connected—and their guilt is making them hold back information you need to grasp the big picture. This is true of Phyllis Haig, and probably Larry Bierly too, and even Crockwell."

"Timothy, if I'm too confused to grasp the big picture, how come you aren't?"

"Probably because I was educated by Jesuits," he said with a chuckle.

His ties to the Mother Church had fallen to all but nil in recent decades, but he still loved to flutter his Georgetown diploma in my face as evidence of both moral and intellectual superiority. He affected a kidding, sometimes even self-deprecatory, tone, but there was much more to it.

"Too bad you didn't marry a Jesuit priest," I said. "Think of the magnificent offspring from such a union as that."

"Oh, don't think I didn't try. Back in Poughkeepsie, it's the one thing the folks could have accepted and understood."

"So tell me this, then, Mr. Sees-All-Knows-All: Why did Vernon Crockwell fire me today?"

He pondered this. "I'm stuck on that one. Though a better question is, Why did Crockwell want to hire you in the first place?"

"Leave it to a Jesuit to unhelpfully answer a question with a question."

"No, really. It is a more useful question."

"You're right, I know. Crockwell kept telling me he'd chosen me on account of my famous super-competence. But he dropped that line after a while. My guess is, the reason he wanted to hire me and the reason he wants to fire me are similar or the same. Whatever they are or it is."

"He's an enigma. An enigma and a—reprehensible character."

"Bierly is easier, of course. He wants me to have Crockwell dragged through the mud for a crime he may have but probably did not commit. Bierly wants this awfully badly, but not so badly that he'll risk my exposing something that went on involving Bierly, Haig, Crockwell and Steven St. James. I'm still at a loss as to what that might be. But if I'm cleverer and luckier talking to Steven St. James than I was the last time I ran into him, maybe we'll soon find out. Anyway, St. James, not having hired me, can't fire me. At least there's that. I'll only have been fired by three people in one day, not four."

"And it's a good thing too," Timmy said. "Four might have put a dent in your self-esteem."

"You never know."

Schuylers Landing was one of those old Hudson River villages whose existence grew precarious in the last century when bridges replaced ferries but which had somehow survived into the age of antique shops, upscale country-charm emporia, and bed-and-breakfasts for purposes of leisure instead of necessity.

According to the waitress in the breezy riverfront café where Timmy and I had a couple of nice Gruyère-and-guacamole panini for lunch, Steven St. James's address was inland, away from the river, and south of the center town on a road off Route 9G.

We found the place with no trouble. St. James lived—Mellors-like—in a converted outbuilding a hundred yards from the house that 175 years earlier would have been the centerpiece of a prosperous landowner's estate. The main house was a brick federal-style manse surrounded by clumps of lavender irises and a couple of immense oak trees that were as graceful as ferns.

St. James's much smaller white clapboard place looked as if it had once been a kind of barn or storage building. It had a board fence around it with wire cattle fencing tacked to the boards, probably to pen in the two dogs that, as Timmy and I stood at the gate, peered at us with interest. One was a big black lab, the other a collie. The gravel parking area outside the fence was empty except for my Mitsubishi. We saw no sign of St. James's VW Rabbit.

"Hello!" I yelled. "Anybody home?"

"These dogs look friendly enough," Timmy said. "Why don't we just walk up and knock at the door?"

"They're friendly, yes. But look—they're slobbering."

"That was a close call, Commando Don."

"Oh, okay, come on."

I unlatched the gate, and Timmy followed me in. I shut the gate and we walked up to St. James's house, the dogs snuffling obsequiously and salivating on our hands.

"We have to remember to get a couple of these," Timmy said. "Uh-huh."

I knocked at the door.

After a moment Timmy said, "It's eerily quiet."

"Well, it's quiet."

I knocked again. When I got no response I walked across the

shaggy lawn and peered through a window. I saw a living room–dining room with a couch, some chairs and tables, a desk with a PC on it, and shelves with a lot of books. I strained to make out the titles, but it was dim in the house and I had no success. The newspaper on the couch appeared to be the *Catskill Daily Mail,* the nearest daily paper. Timmy tried to distract the dogs while I walked around behind the house, but they wanted to come along with me, so we all went, the dogs wetly licking any exposed human skin they could get at.

"These doggies are soon going to need a drink of water," Timmy said.

I peered into a back window and saw a kitchen that was unremarkable. A door leading into it was next to the window, and I turned the knob. Locked.

"I don't think this is legal," Timmy said. "A man's home is his castle. It's English common law, going way back."

A voice said, "Is there something I can help you with perhaps?" The voice was male and its tone unfriendly.

We turned to see a man who was not Steven St. James striding around the corner of the house. He was about seventy and distinguished-looking in a Windsor-ish, end-of-the-line kind of way, and was wearing—weirdly for a sunny afternoon in May—what once had been called, and maybe still was called in the better houses of the Hudson valley, a smoking jacket. His royal-blue display handkerchief matched his ascot.

"Hi, I'm looking for Steven St. James," I said. "I'm Don Strachey and this is Timothy Callahan, and we're old friends of Steven's. Any idea where he is?"

The debonair man had four fingers of his right hand thrust into the pocket of his jacket, like a J. Press model striking a pose in 1932, and he did not remove his hand to shake the one I extended.

"I don't believe Steven was expecting you," the man said coldly. "He never mentioned to me that he was expecting visitors." The dogs paced around restlessly but did not approach the man in the jacket.

"We just decided to pop in at the last minute," Timmy said. "But I guess Steve's not here."

"No, of course Steven is not here. The farm is open now."

The farm. When he didn't elaborate, I said, "You must be Steven's neighbor."

"Yes, I am. Steven is my tenant and my neighbor. And my friend."

"Oh, so you must be—"

"Going now. And so, may I suggest, should you."

"Okay. Love your cologne," I said.

"I beg your pardon?"

"It's the same cologne Steven uses. I got a good whiff of it the other day when I spent some time with Steven in Albany."

His perfect posture weakened a little. "Steven was in Albany?"

"On Friday. How you gonna keep 'em down on the farm after they've seen Central Avenue?"

Timmy glowered at me and began to move around the man in the jacket. The snuffling dogs followed Timmy.

"Tell me your names again," the man said, with much less self-assurance than before, "and I'll let Steven know that you called."

I brought out one of my cards and handed it to him. "Ask him to get in touch with me some time this weekend. Otherwise I can look him up at the farm. Thank you."

"You're welcome." He blushed—*blushed*—and said, "I knew Steven had other friends in Albany. That I understood. I can't object to that. It's just that—I never met any of them before."

Timmy said, "Well, we aren't close friends of Steven or anything. Not that close."

"Oh. I see." But he looked unconvinced.

As we drove away, Timmy said, "You were awfully nasty with that guy."

"He was awfully nasty with us."

"Of course. We were trespassing on his property. Also, he felt threatened. He's probably buying himself—directly or

121

indirectly—a little comfort not otherwise available to someone so geographically and otherwise isolated."

I said, "There were two cars in his driveway, a Continental and a Caddy. I'll bet he's married."

"So?"

"So he's sucking a dick that's been God knows where and bringing who knows what in the way of viruses and bugs and bacteria into that house."

"That is wild, wild speculation, Don. You don't know if that man so much as enjoyed a glass of port with St. James. And you certainly have no idea what St. James does or did in Albany with Bierly or Haig or Crockwell or anybody else."

"No, but on the latter point I do know that when I pressed St. James on the subject, he told me in a panic, 'You don't want to know,' and then he fled."

"You're right. There's that."

"St. James will get the word from Lord Chatterley that I know where he lives and he'll think I know where he works. For those reasons, I think Steven will be ready to enlighten me as to what he says I don't want to know, even though I do, I do."

"I see what you mean when you put it that way. You're kind of pissed off, aren't you?"

"Shouldn't I be?"

"Yes, I understand that. But it's not pretty."

"Something even less pretty got Paul Haig murdered and Larry Bierly shot."

"I guess I should try to keep all that in perspective."

"Do. You can do something else too."

"What?" His tone was apprehensive.

"Write down the plate numbers of the Caddy and the Lincoln. I memorized them." I recited them and Timmy wrote the numbers and letters on the back of an oil-change receipt, which I stuffed in my jacket pocket. On the way back to Albany, neither of us had much to say.

122

17

Roland Stover's apartment was in the basement of a frame house with flaking gray paint on one of the marginal blocks of Morton Avenue across from Lincoln Park. The entrance was from a narrow alleyway between his and the nearly identical house next door, and although the May afternoon was bright, by five-thirty darkness had all but set in down in Stover's depths.

"Oh, we can definitely tell you all there is to know about *those* two," Stover said with a sneer. "Paul Haig and Larry Bierly were a couple of unrepentant buttfuckers, and they both got what they had coming."

"You wouldn't b*elieve* what a disruptive influence those two were in Dr. Crockwell's program," Dean Moody put in. "Larry especially. All that time he was there pretending to want to be sexually repaired like the rest of us, and he was a secret deviant! That big buttfucker was just *toooo* much."

Stover was hulking and wild-eyed, with an erratic crewcut, bad skin, and a Wal-Mart name tag on his white dress shirt. Moody was slight and fluttery and full of manic intensity that must have struck terror in the hearts of the parents he had sued for turning him into a homosexual. After all Mr. and Mrs. Moody had been through, it must have been small compensation that they had gotten to go on Montel.

"Repentance is the way of the Lord," Stover said, jabbing his finger my way. "But never once did those two buttfuckers ask forgiveness for their transgressions. Even in the beginning, I had my suspicions about those two. They said they were unhappy, and they said they were confused, and they were this, and they were that. But never once did those two admit that they were abominations in the eyes of the Lord, abominations to be cast out!"

I said, "Dr. Crockwell's treatment approach wasn't religious in nature, was it? I was under the impression it was more scientific. Secular, anyway."

"Well, yes, that is true," Moody said. "You see, Roland here is an extremely spiritual person, so he tends to see things that way. I'm trying hard to become more spiritual myself. He's helping me. I'd always wanted to get in closer touch with my Lord and Savior, but there were certain things in my life that stood in the way."

I said, "You mean like buttfucking."

They both nodded eagerly. They were seated together on a tattered old plaid couch, Stover's large arm stretched out along the back of the couch behind Moody's little permed hairdo but not, so far as I could see, touching it.

Stover said, "'If a man also lie with mankind, as he lieth with a woman, both of them have committed an abomination: they shall surely be put to death.' Leviticus."

"I suppose it's a big theological question," I said, "as to who shall actually put the buttfuckers to death. I take it that in your view, Roland, it's a dirty theological job, but somebody has to do it. Or have I misunderstood your position?"

"That is an important question," Stover said, poking a thick finger my way again. "And if the liberals didn't control the media and the Supreme Court and the special interests, we'd have capital punishment in this country for sexual deviants. I've read that down in Washington there are buttfuckers under every rock who have Bill Clinton in their pocket and under their thumb. In fact, you might as well just paint the White House lavender."

"Mincin' Bill Clinton," Moody said, waving a mocking limp wrist.

"Clinton is gay? I never heard that."

"Oh, honey, where have you been?" Moody said. "No, really.

124

Gennifer Flowers was one of his beards, and so was that other one."

I said, "I suppose you arrived at this conclusion based on the president's initial position on gays in the military."

"Oh, no," Moody said. "It's not just that. I've seen copies of depositions from men who have slept with Missy Clinton. You can send away for those."

"Well," I said, "this explains a lot."

They both nodded sagely.

"Tell us about your study on deviance," Stover said. "Did you say on the phone that you're doing a deviance survey for Dr. Crockwell?"

"Yes, I am. He couldn't provide me the names of any group members, of course. But Larry Bierly did, and I'm grateful that even though you hate Larry's guts you're still willing to participate in the study."

"Will you be asking questions about our former sexual practices?" Moody said.

They both looked expectant, but I said, "No, it's treatment programs that I'm most interested in. I'm doing a study on comparative methods of treatment for deviance."

They both said, "Oh."

"I'd like to hear more about Dr. Crockwell's program from the patient's point of view. The dynamic of the group you were in interests me especially."

They both looked bored. Group dynamics was not what they hoped to discuss with me.

"The group part wasn't all that great," Moody said. "I mean, it was important—learning guy things and all. But for Roland and I, the individual treatment Dr. Crockwell had to offer was what really turned things around for us."

"What did the individual treatment consist of?"

"Aversion therapy, it's called. Where the incorrect sexual conditioning that was done by our parents is corrected by punishing wrong sexual thoughts and rewarding right ones."

"Zapping the demons," Stover added. "Casting out the evil spirits."

"Electric shocks were used?"

"Yeah, everybody went over to Dr. Crockwell's three times a week," Moody said. "You could do it two ways. You'd get wired up with electrodes and look at slides of naked women and hot guys. If you were on automatic, you'd get zapped whenever the picture showed humpy guys but not when it was tits and pussy. Or you could do it yourself—zap yourself when guys were on and you started getting hard. If you stayed stiff, you could turn up the dial till it really hurt a whole lot, and that usually did the trick."

"It's remarkable," I said, "that so simple a procedure could actually reverse sexual orientation."

"It's not just the therapy," Moody said. "It's a deep commitment, too, to normalcy."

Stover added, "The Lord would have made Adam and Steve, not Adam and Eve, if he had meant for men to fuck each other in the butt."

"Are you ever tempted to backslide?" I asked. "No pun intended."

"Once in a while," Moody said, looking troubled. "Dr. Crockwell told us this would occur in some patients. But Roland and I have figured out ways of dealing with that."

They both looked at me uncertainly.

I said, "How?"

"We look at dirty pictures together," Stover said. "Or once in a while videos."

I said, "I guess that falls under the heading of giving the devil his due."

Stover looked at me suspiciously, and Moody wasn't sure he liked the sound of that either.

I said, "How do you create the electric shocks? I hope you're not risking death or serious injury with a toaster or anything like that, guys."

"Oh, no, no," Stover said. "We use a safe device like Dr. Crockwell's. The one we have is called a Lustbuster. You can get them

126

through Christian religious-supply catalogs. Would you like to see it?"

"We could demonstrate how it's used," Moody said, "if you'd be interested for your survey."

My impulse was to dive through a window. But that might have been seen as overreacting, so I said, "The device sounds interesting, but I'd like to know more about the group therapy sessions. It must have been difficult having men in the group who resisted treatment at one level or another, unlike you eager beavers."

"I can tell you it was a real bitch," Moody said. "You just felt like you were surrounded by traitors."

I said, "That wasn't true for the first eight months, was it? I thought Larry and Paul pretty much observed the spirit of the occasion until they decided to leave. And that all happened in just one session last fall."

"Oh, I'm sure that's what Miss La-di-da Larry would have you believe," Moody said. "That they were such angels. Well, my dear, I can assure you that they were not."

"Dr. Crockwell was there to help us with our sexual dysfunctions," Stover said, panting and jabbing his finger. "And Paul and Larry were always bringing all kinds of problems that had nothing to do with deviancy—drinking and drugs and money problems and stuff like that. As for those, we were there to discuss just one topic," Stover said, brandishing a finger.

And I knew by then what that was. I said, "Who had the alcohol and drug problem?"

"Paul was an alcoholic and Larry was a druggie," Moody said. "They were always dishing and criticizing each other, and one thing I hold against Dr. Crockwell is, he let them go on like that too much. We weren't there to deal with topics like that, and we didn't need to hear it. Like Roland says, we'd paid our money to talk about one thing."

"But wouldn't you say that drugs and alcohol are a common way for men unhappy with their sexuality to cope with it, or avoid coping with it? It's often part of the picture that has to be addressed."

127

"But not always bickering the way those two did," Moody said. "Take it to AA or NA, Grace, or keep it on the street."

"I'd heard Paul was an alcoholic," I said, "but I wasn't aware of Larry's drug problem. What kind of drugs did he do?"

Stover looked blank, but Moody's recall on the subject was instant. "He was into both Ecstasy and acid, I know. They had a real catfight over it right in the group one time, and Paul accused Larry of spending money that he needed for his business on drugs. Of course, Paul was the one who was always in trouble over money, and Larry reminded him of it and told him to just butt out."

"It didn't surprise me one bit," Stover said, "when I heard that Paul ended up dead in the gutter. Since he had turned his back on righteousness, it was the best thing he could do for himself."

I said, "Paul may not have killed himself. He may have been murdered. The police are looking into the possibility."

Neither of them reacted dramatically to this news. Moody pursed his lips and got a quizzical look, and Stover just kept looking hard and mean and unaffected by the fate of a man he didn't approve of.

"Who do they think did it?" Moody finally said.

"They don't know. Who can you think of who might have had a reason to kill Paul? Or hated him enough to want to?"

"It was probably queer-boy Bierly," Stover said. Moody pondered this briefly and then nodded.

"Why do you think Larry would kill Paul? They had their disagreements, but they were lovers, after all."

"That's exactly what I mean," Stover snarled. "Homos are unstable people. You keep taking it up the butt, sooner or later you'll crack. It happens all the time. Don't you watch Pat Robertson?"

I said I'd only tuned in briefly. "What about Dr. Crockwell?" I asked. "He's a suspect in the eyes of some. And he was certainly upset with Paul for leaving the group."

"Oh, Mary! Gimme a break, puh-*leeze!*" Moody squealed.

"Who's going around saying such a thing?" Stover roared. "The idea of slandering a man of Dr. Crockwell's standing in the community is character assassination."

I said, "Crockwell doesn't have an alibi, either. On the Thursday night Paul Haig died, Dr. Crockwell was alone in his office until after midnight, he says. Interestingly, the same is true for last Thursday night, when someone shot Larry Bierly in the Millpond Mall parking lot."

They both got an I-smell-a-rat look. "Then maybe it was one of Dr. Crockwell's patients or former patients," Moody said, "and they were trying to pin something on him. Everybody who ever went to him knew Dr. Crockwell worked all by himself in his office on Thursday night. It's when you could call there and he'd answer the phone at night instead of you getting his answering machine."

"Is there anyone in the group who might have wanted to do that?" I asked. "I mean, set Crockwell up?"

"Dr. Crockwell was a beloved guy figure to all of us," Stover harrumphed. "He was a role model and a pal. Except to Larry and Paul, of course, those Judases who betrayed us all."

"Anyway," Moody said, "Dr. Crockwell had three other groups going all the time, ten homos in a group. And if you count people from other years, hundreds of ex-gays must know about his Thursday-night routine."

With a sinking feeling, I said, "I guess that would be true. Is either of you acquainted with a man by the name of Steven St. James?"

Moody shook his head, and Stover said, "No, is he a saint?"

I said I didn't know for sure, but I doubted it.

18

On Sunday morning, cool and rainy, Timmy had gone out and come back with bagels and the *Times,* and the kitchen was an aromatic Malabar Coast as he prepared his masala tea. Perhaps on that day in Visakhapatnam, twenty-six years after Timmy's Peace Corps leave-taking, an American ritual he had left behind was being reenacted similarly—a middle-aged Indian was sitting and picking the lint off his socks or whatever. I preferred what Timmy had brought home to what I imagined he had left behind. But my imagination in these matters was limited, as I was reminded whenever Timmy's Peace Corps crowd got together and conversed in the patois of their exotic youth with its references to chicken sexing and blood meal, and place names that sounded like long, quick combinations of vowels, consonants and simmering lentils.

I got on the phone. I reached my Department of Motor Vehicles contact at home. He called back three minutes later and, having spoken with a member of the weekend crew keeping an eye on the department's computer system, informed me that the two cars in Lord Chatterley's driveway, the Caddy and the Continental, were registered to Mr. Emil Provost, of that address in Schuylers Landing. The name rang no bell, but why would it?

I couldn't think of anybody I knew in Schuylers Landing, so I called a friend who worked for the New York State Historical Society and asked her about a member of the landed gentry in Schuylers Landing named Emil Provost. She had never heard of him, but she knew who to call downriver. Ten minutes later I had been informed that: Emil Provost was the surviving patriarch of an old Hudson River family that had made a lot of early money in canal shipping and later money in railroads; Provost and his wife, Ina, had two daughters and a son, all living in Greene County and involved in banking and real estate; both Emil and Ina Provost were patrons of worthy causes, she historical preservation, he naturalist organizations. He was also part-owner of the Hudson Valley Game Farm, I was told, and I thought: "farm." Steven St. James had not been at home on Saturday because "the farm is open now."

I phoned the game farm, a touristy zoo and wild-animal preserve off the thruway, and asked for St. James—I did not slip and call him "Mellors"—and was told that he was not available at the moment, but would I like to leave a message? I said no thanks.

When I'd gotten home Saturday night I found a message on my machine from my credit-check contact. She had informed me, with full particulars, that Larry Bierly's financial situation was stable, that his business financing was stretched to the limit but his cash flow was sufficient to keep him afloat. Paul Haig, on the other hand, had been on the edge of financial collapse when he died. As Bierly had told me truthfully, it was only his personal intercession after Haig's death that had saved Beautiful Thingies from being snatched back by Haig's creditors.

I said to Timmy, "I've got it."

" 'It'?" He was absorbed in the *Times* crossword puzzle, and I knew I would have access to only about a tenth of his brain until he had either completed the puzzle or, after inner pain, made the mature decision to put the puzzle aside unfinished and resume his life.

"I think I know why Paul died."

He looked at me interestedly across the dining room table, his pencil still poised. "Why?"

"He died because he was trying to blackmail someone to get hold of enough money to save his business. As you theorized, he had gone to his mother for money and she had turned him down. That's why she's alternately guilt-ridden and delusionary over what deep in her heart she thinks of as Paul's suicide—his suicide over impending financial ruin. But Haig told Bierly a week before he died that his financial troubles were over, that he'd come up with a way to pay off his debt. He didn't tell Bierly how he was raising the cash, because he couldn't—it was illegal."

Timmy put his pencil down.

"The other reason he couldn't tell Bierly was, Bierly probably knew the person Haig was blackmailing and even the guilty secret that made the blackmail possible. Had he been informed of the blackmail attempt, Bierly might have objected—on ethical grounds, or even fear of his own involvement and exposure."

Timmy said, "That's plausible, but where's the evidence of any of it?"

"I haven't found any yet. But get this: Bierly, Crockwell, St. James and St. James's landlord—whose name is Emil Provost, I now know—all seem to have been mixed up in something together none of them wants to talk about. That thing is what Haig was using to blackmail one of them. The next question is, Which one? Bierly, of course, was not a candidate for blackmail, because in March he was still Haig's friend, if no longer lover, and anyway he had no ready cash. St. James is an unlikely target; he drives an old Rabbit and works in a game park with—by the smell of him—farm animals. He's not at all a good blackmailee.

"Crockwell is a possibility. He must have a few bucks in the bank that he's extracted over the years from his bevies of repentant buttfuckers. Though if Crockwell was being blackmailed by Haig, and then killed Haig to shut him up, why would Crockwell hire me and risk my uncovering three ugly truths—the blackmail, the thing that made the blackmail possible, and the murder?"

Timmy said, "That leaves—Provost? That sad old man?"

"Emil Provost is wealthy. There's a lot of oldish money in the family that appears not to have been misspent or otherwise dissipated. He's an ideal blackmail target."

He looked at me skeptically. "Do you really think that decrepit old aristocrat could have killed Paul Haig?"

"Haig wasn't strangled with some goon's bare hands," I said.

132

"Somebody he obviously knew somehow induced him to start drinking again and got him drunk and then dissolved the Elavil in his Scotch. Anybody of any age or background could have accomplished that."

"Sure—anybody who is completely without morals or human feelings. That old guy didn't strike me that way at all."

"Timothy, not every murderer looks like Charles Manson. You're talking as if you don't own a television set or read a daily newspaper. Dear hearts and gentle people who live and love in your hometown can have murder in their hearts. It happens somewhere every day."

After a moment he said, "That's true, sure. But I don't think that old guy is one of those. For him, murder would be—you know. In poor taste."

"That's exactly my point," I said. "Provost is a pillar of his community. He has everything to lose. As a blackmail target, he's a natural."

"He was cool and condescending to you, so that makes him a murderer? Nah, I don't believe it."

"That's not what I said."

"Anyway, what could they all have been mixed up in that Provost would actually kill somebody over to stop it from coming out?"

I said, "I don't know."

"You don't have a clue?"

"No."

"That's a problem with your theory."

"It might have something to do with drugs," I said, without much conviction. "Moody and Stover, the low-voltage fetishists, told me Bierly and Haig used to argue about their drug habits in the therapy group—Haig's alcohol dependency and Bierly's penchant for street drugs. I'll have to look into that one some more. Otherwise, I won't know what they're all hiding until one of them decides to tell me. Bierly's a possibility. Once he understands that his and the others' dirty secret may have led to blackmail and Haig's murder, that should loosen him up."

133

"And if it doesn't?"

"I can try the same approach with both Crockwell and St. James."

"But," Timmy said, "if all of these people were involved in something that made them vulnerable to blackmail, wouldn't they already have speculated on the possibility that Paul had threatened one of the others with exposure and was killed for it? And thinking that, they haven't come forward so far for the same reason they won't in the future: Exposure of the mysterious foul goings-on would ruin their lives too."

"There is that," I said. "But there's another possibility, too, for finding out what Paul Haig might have been mixed up in with Bierly, Crockwell and St. James. There's another person he might have confided in."

"Not Mom?"

"Not a chance, is my guess. According to Bierly, the Haigs not only did not confide in one another, they lied to one another habitually. No, the man Haig may have trusted with the information that was so volatile that it got him killed is the man he went to for relief from the anxiety that that information and other stresses in his life were causing him. That man is Dr. Glen Snyder, the Ballston Spa psychiatrist Haig went to for the month before he died and who prescribed the Elavil that killed him."

"Do you think he'll talk to you? It's hard to imagine he would."

"Not," I said, "if I just walk in off the street. He might open up, however, if he is urged to do so by someone whose good opinion he needs and who is the family member who sent Paul Haig to him in the first place."

"Phyllis Haig. Back to her again. The client from hell."

"Oh, I've got plenty of those. Or did."

134

19

Sunday afternoon I drove over to Albany Med. I talked my way past the guard and into Bierly's room, but when I got there he refused to speak with me. I told him, "I think Paul was killed by someone he was trying to blackmail. It had to do with whatever you and Paul and Crockwell and St. James and Emil Provost were mixed up in together. If you want Paul's killer brought to justice, you've got to open up about this."

But he had already buzzed for the nurse, and when she arrived Bierly was looking at me peculiarly and slowly shaking his head.

"Just leave me alone, will you, please?" he said, not at all Garbo-like—Victor Mature–like was closer to it. The nurse said I would have to go, so I did.

Back on Crow Street, I sat down by the phone. Crockwell's home number was unlisted, and his machine answered at his office. I got no answer at the St. James number; he was probably still at the game farm. I started to dial Phyllis Haig, but checked my watch—1:40—and figured I might make out better at that time of day if I met her face-to-face. Timmy had gone off with some friends to a lecture at SUNY on the evils of the Guatemalan military. I drove up to Latham for my own encounter with a kind of human-being-as-banana-republic.

"I don't want to talk to you, I said you are *fired*—F-I-R-E-E-D. Can't you understand *English?* Do I have to call a *cop?"* She was standing barricade-like in her front doorway, a low glass in her hand.

I said, "Look, Paul did not commit suicide. You were right

when you called me the first time. I keep trying to tell you, Phyllis, that there is evidence pointing to the likelihood that Paul was murdered. I need to talk to you about it, and I need your help in identifying Paul's killer."

She looked more worn out than relieved by this assertion, as if the thing she was least able to cope with now was additional thought.

"Oh, Christ on a crutch," she finally said resignedly. "Come on in and let me fix you a drink."

I followed her through the foyer of a rambling split-level house full of horsey prints and Duncan Phyfe reproductions of unvarying constricted good taste, the sort of decor Joseph Stalin might have chosen for the Kremlin had he been from Connecticut. The one touch of modern-day-Haig authenticity in the place, and of life, was Phyllis Haig herself. She'd gotten her makeup to fit almost exactly over its intended place on her face, and she had on a pair of silky pale blue slacks that were casually hippy and an orange blouse with plenty of demurely rouged decolletage.

She said, "We better head for the den if we know what's good for us."

What was good for Phyllis was a cigarette and a refill, and I had a reactionary but well-chilled Coors.

"I don't know why you're still pestering me," she said, draping herself across a chintz couch. I chose the well-worn manly leather chair facing her that must have been her late husband's seat. "You keep missing the point, Donald, that I've had it up to here with you and with this whole goddamn stinking load of crap. I should never have called you in the first place. I should have gone to Arizona with Helen Small when she tried to get me to hop on a plane and blow this Popsicle stick. But no, I didn't listen to Helen. Just to get even with that stupid little pansy Larry Bierly, I had to start picking at scabs and opening up running sores and dredging up a lot of ugliness and heartbreak. Well, I learned my lesson on this one, Don, that's for goddamned certain. Never again, never again. Not ever, ever, ever."

136

What was she trying to say? "I'm a little hazy on that, Phyllis. Never again what?"

"Some people can get away with murder and there's nothing you can do about it. My husband told me a hundred times if he told me once, when you run into one of those people who can get away with anything they damn well please, don't screw around with them. It's just not worth it."

"Who do you think is getting away with murder?" I said, and as I said it, it suddenly sounded as wacky to me as it must have sounded to Phyllis Haig.

"Why, Larry Bierly! What the hell do you think I've been telling you for the last five days, for chrissakes?" She stared at me as if I were armed and dangerous.

I said, "I got the wrong impression from something you said over the phone, Phyllis. I'm sorry about the confusion. I misunderstood and got the idea from the way you reacted to some things I said about Paul's financial situation at Beautiful Thingies that you felt you were somehow responsible for his death."

She sagged. "Oh, that's what you thought?"

"I'm sorry."

She blew smoke over her left shoulder and then peered at me through narrowed eyes. After a moment she said, "Well, it's the goddamned truth."

"What's the truth?"

She took in another lungful for strength. "It's true that I'm partly responsible for my son's death, goddamnit to hell."

When she just sat watching me with a look of defiance tinged with despair, I said, "In what way are you partly responsible?"

She shuddered and then shook her head. "Why am I telling you this?"

"Because you have to tell someone, Phyllis."

That got a snort. "What bullshit. I know verbal diarrhea is in style, but I've done without it for fifty-some years and I don't intend to take up the disgusting habit now. No, I'm spilling my guts to you, Don, because I think you are a pathetically naive man and I want to educate you. What you can learn from me will come in handy in your line of work. And I won't even charge you for it."

"Thank you, Phyllis."

She ingested and inhaled. The drinking was painful to watch, but she smoked with such fierce pleasure that it took me back to when I was young and easy under the apple boughs and constantly sucking on a Chesterfield or an Old Gold and finding happiness if not health in every drag.

Abruptly, she said tightly, "Paul came to me for money. I refused to give it to him."

She watched me for a reaction, but I offered none.

She went on. "After Paul left Vernon Crockwell's program, Crockwell called me. He advised me to shut Paul out—disown him, is what Crockwell was saying, even though he never used the ugly word. He said if Paul wanted anything from me to make sure I gave it to him only if Paul first agreed to go back into Crockwell's program. He also said it would be best if Paul started fresh, without Larry Bierly, because Bierly was probably a hopeless case, a man who wanted to be a pervert. Crockwell said this approach might be a tough row to hoe for me, but it was in Paul's best interest in the long run."

Another gulp of whatever was in the glass.

"I'd already paid Crockwell over eight K," She said. "And I figured a man who can rake in that kind of money from zinging people with cattle prods, or whatever it is he does, and getting them to think normal smutty thoughts, must know what he's doing. So when Paul asked me for sixty thousand dollars in March, I said I'd give it to him only after he went back into Crockwell's program and finished it and Crockwell personally guaranteed me that Paul had come out normal. That's a lot of money for a warranty, but normalcy is worth money."

I said, "But Paul didn't accept the offer."

"No," she said grimly. "He said he might go back to Crockwell sometime—he'd have to think about that. Apparently he still had dick on his mind. He'd already started seeing Glen Snyder, who'd

138

put him on the Elavil, but that was only making him feel less anxious, not more normal. The main thing was, Paul said, he needed the sixty thousand right away, for business reasons."

"But not," I said, "Larry Bierly's business reasons. You told me on Wednesday that it was Larry Bierly's business that was in trouble. But you misspoke yourself, I take it."

She sprayed smoke my way, then shrugged. "Whatever. The point is, Donald—if you are the least bit interested in the point— the point is, Paul needed the money sooner than I was willing to give it to him. And when I begged off, he—he did something dumb. I saw Paul a week later and Paul said he no longer needed the sixty K and that he had come up with another source. But it wasn't a way of raising cash that Paul should ever have used."

This left her mute and looking a little queasy. I said, "I assume you mean blackmail."

She stiffened. "How did you know?"

"I was told blackmail had been used previously by a member of your family."

"Who told you that?"

"Paul told Larry Bierly, who told me, that your husband once tried to blackmail a public official and this became known."

She deflated, looking glum. "That's the way some people interpreted the situation at the time—people who had their own reasons for seeing my husband left out in the cold in a certain investment situation. Paul was young at the time, but Deedee told him about it, and Paul somehow got it into his head that this was a viable way of doing business that you can get away with. If he'd still been alive, my husband would have set Paul straight on that one, that's for goddamn sure. But Lew was gone and Paul had this idea. So when he came around for a handout in March and I said no dice, not until you're normal, he came back a week later and said not to worry, he was raising the cash another way, using 'an old Haig family tradition,' he called it. Knowing how kids' minds work, I knew exactly what that was supposed to mean."

"Did you ask him what it meant?"

"We discussed it. I told him he was asking for trouble."

139

"But Paul made plain to you that he was blackmailing someone to raise the sixty thousand dollars he said he needed to save his business? That was spelled out?"

"It was clear enough." She straightened up and lit another Camel Light with the butt end of the last one.

"Did he say who he was blackmailing and what information he was using to do it with?"

"No, but I knew. I knew."

"How did you know?"

"Well, who the hell else would it be except that conniving little sexual deviate that had ruined Paul's life and kept him from being the real man he could have been if that treacherous little cocksucker hadn't waved his pretty dick under Paul's nose and gotten him all sexually confused again? That's who!"

Not this again. I said, "Phyllis, surely you aren't referring to Larry Bierly."

"Of course I am!"

"But why would Paul blackmail Bierly? First of all, he was his friend. Secondly, Bierly had no money. He was in debt himself."

She cocked an eyebrow and gave me her oh-you-poor-naive-kid look. "Donald, sometimes you do amaze me. To think I almost paid you good money to work for me for—a gazillion dollars or whatever it was you wanted to hold me up for. Now pay attention, Elmer Fudd, here's the deal. Those two weren't friends. They were two queers. It was all sex. Buttfucking and whatnot. This is not healthy, and that's why homosexuals are always having catfights and can't be trusted and will never get along. It's a sickness. People of this type are not capable of true, lasting friendships with other men."

She watched me, gauging my reaction. I said, "The empirical evidence shows that you are badly mistaken, Phyllis. But do go on."

She raised her drink, acknowledging what she seemed to interpret as my conceding a point. "And anyway," she said, "even if fag-boy Bierly had no cash, he had the equity in his business and

140

he could have raised the money. And he would have done it too, you can bet your bottom dollar on that."

I swigged from my glass of beer. I tried to imagine what it must have been like growing up with Phyllis Haig, and my heart went out anew for her lost son, his sanity squeezed and beaten out of him long before he knew it.

I said, "Why would Larry Bierly have sold his business and let Paul blackmail him, Phyllis?"

She said, "He had pictures."

"Paul did?"

"He told me he had photographs."

"Of what?"

She gave her head a firm shake. "Paul never told me and, believe me, I did not want to know."

"He said he had incriminating or damaging photos of Larry Bierly? He specifically mentioned Bierly's name?"

"He might not have mentioned Bierly's name. I forget. But to me it was as plain as the nose on your face."

"Did Paul say where he kept the photos?"

"Why would he tell me?"

"Did he say whether there were extra copies, or negatives?"

"We didn't go into it. I wasn't the least bit interested. I told Paul I thought the whole thing was dangerous and ridiculous and dumb, and he ought to have his head examined."

"Then why, Phyllis, if you tried to discourage Paul from blackmailing someone—someone who probably murdered Paul to get hold of the incriminating photos and to silence him—why, then, do you say you are partly responsible for his death?"

Looking desolate, she said, almost inaudibly, "Because the last time I saw Paul, he asked me for the money one last time. He didn't want to be a blackmailer like his father, he said."

"And?"

"I refused. I told him I would only give him the money if he went back to Crockwell."

"Oh."

She gazed over at me out of her ruined face. "If I had given Paul the money—he'd still be alive."

"This is possible."

"He'd still be queer, but at least he wouldn't be dead. There'd be hope for Paul."

I said, "Why didn't you tell me this before? On Wednesday, you left this crucial information, about the blackmail, out of your story of what happened, Phyllis."

She looked at me hopelessly. She said, "It was too touchy. I hate all this. I just hate it."

"I guess so."

"With the Haigs, blackmail is a touchy subject."

"It sounds that way," I said. "Phyllis, I think you owe it to your son's memory to do what you can to see that the killer is caught and convicted."

"I suppose so."

"I'm going to continue to investigate. You can either pay me or not pay me, that's up to you. But I'll need your help."

"All right. All right, all right. Shit."

"Paul may have confided in Glen Snyder while he was in therapy during the six weeks before he died," I said. "Snyder is probably still under the impression that Paul committed suicide. I want your permission to interview Snyder and lay out the evidence that Paul was murdered, and I want you to urge Snyder to tell me anything relevant that Paul confided to him during those six weeks. It's unlikely Paul would have discussed the actual blackmail with Dr. Snyder—that's a crime, after all. But he could well have talked about activities of his own that would have provided him with the information—and the photos—that he ended up using in the blackmail attempt. Will you do that?"

Suddenly exhausted, she put her drink aside and laid her cigarette in an ashtray full of butts, several smoldering. She was starting to nod off. She said, "I'll do what I can. But I don't think I can pay you. You charge an arm and a leg, you know, and I'm going to have to paint the house this summer."

"We can talk about that later, Phyllis." I meant when she was sober, provided I could locate a window of opportunity.

Blinking and trying to remain conscious, she said, "How the hell did all this crazy shit happen?"

After a moment, I said it probably went way back. But by then she had begun to snore.

20

I managed to get Larry Bierly on the phone at Albany Med. He said, "There *are no pictures.*"

"But Paul told his mother there are."

"But I'm telling you there *are no pictures.* And anyway, Strachey, you are completely off base."

I said, "Where are Paul's personal belongings?"

"I've got some, Phyllis has some, and a lot we gave away."

"I'd like to have a look at what you've got. If there's nothing there, there's nothing there. But humor me in this, Larry."

"No, I will not. I'm telling you, Strachey, it's all a waste of time, what you're doing. Just drop it. It's not worth it."

"After Paul died and you went into his apartment, was there any indication the place had been searched?"

A little silence. "I don't think so. But I do know this for sure: there *are no pictures.*"

"Pictures of what?"

"I can't tell you. If I could, I would. But it has nothing to do with Paul's death—that I am one hundred percent certain of. Why the fuck can't you just take my word about this, Strachey?"

"But Larry, if you know exactly what I'm talking about that there are no pictures of, and if it's so sensitive a subject that you refuse to tell me about it, then why couldn't Paul have tried to blackmail someone with this information and that person killed him to shut him up?"

Bierly said nothing, but I could hear him breathing, and I thought I could almost, but not quite, hear him thinking.

144

I said, "Could Paul have been blackmailing Emil Provost?"

"Who?"

"Steven St. James's gentleman friend."

No response.

I said, "Did it have anything to do with drugs?"

Another silence.

"Two members of the therapy group told me you and Paul used to argue about his alcohol intake and your regular use of recreational street drugs, namely acid and Ecstasy. Were drugs involved in the blackmail situation or actions?"

"Shit!" he said, and his phone came crashing down.

With the dial tone I now had, I considered calling him again but decided instead to let him cool off. After all, he wasn't going anywhere.

Crockwell still wasn't answering his phone, and neither was Steven St. James. I did reach Phyllis Haig, who by late afternoon was up and around again. She remembered the gist of our conversation and said she'd call Dr. Glen Snyder in Ballston Spa and give her okay for him to talk to me about Paul and his brief course of therapy with Snyder in February and March. I told her to emphasize to Snyder that it now seemed likely Paul had not committed suicide—no therapist likes the idea of a patient in his or her care rejecting life and the world and the therapist—and that murder was more likely. An hour later, Snyder called me and said he could talk to me Monday evening at eight if I'd drive up to his Ballston Spa office. I said I would.

Timmy and I dined at the new Vietnamese place on Madison, and I told him about my visit with Phyllis Haig, her confirmation of my suspicions about blackmail and her revelation about incriminating photographs.

"This is getting pretty racy," he said.

"Why 'racy'? That's a term with sexual connotations."

"I don't know. It's just that blackmail photos are often sexual."

"But it's hard to imagine the parties involved in this—the ones St. James said I 'don't want to know' what they were up to together—combining for anything sexual. Not Crockwell, anyway.

The others conceivably, but not the cure-a-fag high priest of the Hudson Valley. Of course, Emil Provost still looks like an ideal candidate for sexual blackmail—old-crust family man and all that."

"So you still think that old guy who goes around in a smoking jacket in the middle of May, and who probably couldn't find his way around Albany without a chauffeur and a valet, drove up alone to Albany in March and somehow got Paul Haig alone in his apartment and forced him to drink a bottle of Scotch laced with enough Elavil to kill him? Don, it's farfetched."

I said, "Maybe St. James was in on it. He helped."

"That's a little more plausible."

"It's one of the possibilities I might ask St. James about. I'm going to take a chance and drive down there after dinner. St. James ought to be resting at home tonight after a long day at the animal farm. Do you want to come along?"

"I'll pass. But good luck. You'd better take some Mace along, in case those wild dogs are on the loose again."

"I'll just use psychology. Like we did yesterday."

"In case he asks, who are you going to tell St. James your client is on this case?"

"Good question, Timothy. It will give me something to think about on the way down—and on the way back too, if I have to."

WAMC had pushed back the Sunday-night jazz shows yet another half-hour to make way for a program of Irish music—not Irish drama, mind you, or Irish literature, but Irish *music*. What was next, Irish cuisine? Heading down the thruway, I played an old Horace Silver tape. The road was still wet in spots, but the sky had cleared and stars were breaking out across the purple dusk. Traffic was heavy with weekenders heading back to the city. The flow slowed to a crawl in spots on account of bridge reconstruction. Bridge rebuilding had been popular in New York State since the collapse of a thruway span in the eighties killed several motorists—though when Senate Republicans complained of high construction costs, Timmy said maybe they could just put up

146

signs along certain stretches of the thruway that said "Falling Bridge Zone."

I pulled into St. James's parking area at nine-ten next to his old Rabbit. Lights were on in his little house. I walked up to his front door and knocked.

St. James opened the door in the company of the two snuffling dogs, who came at me sniffing and licking.

"Hi, Steven, I'm Don Strachey, and I'm a private investigator. We met on Friday at Albany Med."

"I remember you. My landlord said you came here yesterday. How did you even know where I lived?" He looked alarmed but not panic-stricken. Just out of the shower, apparently, he was barefoot in jeans and a white T-shirt. Auburn hair curled up out of the neck of his shirt in the front and down over his neck in the back. He looked nice and smelled good, the same cologne as the other day.

I said, "I'd like to talk to you about a case of blackmail involving Paul Haig, you, Emil Provost, Larry Bierly and Vernon Crockwell. Have you got a few minutes?"

He took this in with what looked like fear mixed with bewilderment. But there was no indication he felt cornered and might try to bolt.

"I can't believe this," was all he said, as he shook his head. "I just can't believe this."

"You can't believe what?"

"That I'm being dragged into—whatever I'm being dragged into. Did they find out who shot Larry?"

"Not yet."

"I called him at the hospital yesterday. I had to work and I couldn't get up to see him. I asked Larry about you, and he did say he knew you. But he said he didn't think you would bother me, and if you did I shouldn't give you the time of day. So—no. No, you can't come in. I'm sorry."

"Look," I said, "it's either me or the Albany cops. Take your pick. Believe me, I'm preferable. I could go to them and tell them all I know about you and Emil and Larry and Paul and all of it, and

147

let them apply their customary thumbscrews. From me, though, you might get a little understanding or even sympathy. Unless, of course, you don't deserve it."

St. James looked aghast, the desired effect, and the panic I saw in him in the hospital parking lot was staring to show up again in his eyes. Finally, he shook his head once, as if to make me disappear, and when he saw that I hadn't, he said, "I guess we'd better sit down."

I followed him inside, and when the dogs kept at me, St. James said, "Mike—Bob—lay down."

I said, "Your dogs aren't named after opera characters."

"Oh, no. No, they're not."

"Good for you."

"Mike is named after Michelangelo, and Bob is named for Robert Taylor, the actor and for many years Barbara Stanwyck's husband."

"Ah."

"A former roommate named them."

I sat on the couch and St. James sat across from me in an easy chair in front of the bookshelves I'd seen the day before through the window. The books were mostly on zoology and animal husbandry, but one section was devoted to Hollywood bios.

I said, "I guess you can change roommates, but you can't change your dogs' names."

"You can change dogs' names," St. James said, "if you do it gradually over time—there's no harm in it. But I really don't see any reason to." Mike and Bob lay on the rug on either side of St. James, peering over at me and emitting fluids in various states.

"Steven," I said, "it's time to fess up."

He stared at me. "You said something about Emil, and about blackmail. What on earth does that mean?"

"I think that's something you need to tell me."

He kept staring and was starting to sweat. He was going to need a fresh T-shirt. "I just don't get it, is all that I'm saying. What does Emil have to do with it?"

I said, "There are pictures—photographs."

"There are?"

"Paul Haig had them."

"But who took the pictures? And what does Emil have to do with it all?"

I said, "Are you telling me Emil wasn't involved?"

"Of course not. Don't be ridiculous."

"This would be easier to sort out," I said, "and a lot less confusing for everybody concerned if I knew what the hell it is we are talking about, Steven. On Friday, I asked you what you and Crockwell and Bierly and Haig were mixed up in together, and you said, quote, 'You don't want to know.' But I do. Because it now appears that Paul was trying to blackmail one of the participants in the you-don't-want-to-know business, and he may well have been murdered in order to halt the blackmail and shut him up. Neither Bierly nor Crockwell has yet explained to me what was going on among you, so it's up to you to break the logjam. Either that or the lot of you are likely to be hauled in by the Albany Police Department, which will read you your Miranda rights and then start peeling your skin off in strips—figuratively speaking, of course, though you'll hardly notice the difference."

He was shaking his head again, not in denial but in apparent disbelief. "This is incredible. I never wanted to do it in the first place. It wasn't my idea. But I was high and I just—went along."

"Along with what?"

"We did something that I knew was wrong."

"Uh-huh."

"We'd never have done it if we hadn't been flying high. I know that's no excuse."

"No, it never is."

"But there was nobody to say, Wait a minute, no, this is crazy, it's cruel, it's torture, it's—illegal. We were all under the influence—a terrible, terrible mistake."

"You and Paul and Larry and—?"

"The three of us."

"No Emil?"

He laughed once. "God, no. Emil? Where did you get an idea like that?"

I could no longer remember. I said, "I'm not sure. But aren't you—involved with him? Look, I'm gay and you don't have to hold back. I'm hip to these things."

"Oh, well, I'm glad you're hip," St. James said, with a Mellors-like sneer. "I knew you were gay—Larry told me—but I didn't know you were hip too. That makes this whole thing so much easier."

I said, "So you and Emil aren't an occasional item?"

" 'An occasional item.' Such a sensitive way of putting it, Strachey. No, we're not. Emil happens to be in love with me. He sometimes imagines that I'm in love with him—which I'm not—and that I hold my passions in check because he's married and because of class differences. But it's all in his head. I haven't done a thing to either lead him on or to make him believe I'm abstaining from sex with him for any reason other than that I don't happen to be interested. I do like him—he's a sweet old guy from another age who's as gay as I am but who grew up differently and who's trying to find a way to be true to his sexual nature, but can't. Sometimes I wish I was attracted to him, because he's a decent man and deserves better. But I'm not attracted, and our relationship exists entirely within Emil's fantasy life—which is real enough to him that he's powerfully jealous of the other men in my life, real and imagined."

I said, "I misunderstood the situation. Sorry."

"Oh, no problem, no problem at all. God."

"So Emil wasn't involved in—'it.' Who was?"

"I told you. Larry and Paul and I. And of course Dr. Crockwell."

"Right." I waited. He looked at me and said nothing, his scent becoming Mellors-like again.

"Paul and Larry were very, very angry," he said tightly. "Especially Larry."

"At Crockwell."

He nodded.

150

"So?"

St. James started breathing hard. "I think—I think I could go to prison for this," he said.

"You all got high and you did something to Crockwell?"

He nodded.

"Which was?"

He said, "I—I can't tell you."

"Why?"

"We all swore we'd never tell."

"Even Crockwell?"

"Especially Crockwell. He said he'd never press charges if we all kept our mouths shut."

"Jesus, did you rape him?"

Now he grimaced. "God, no! What kind of people do you think we are?"

"The kind that could go to prison for whatever you did do. You just said so, Steven."

"Yes, but—no, I would never do a thing like that. And neither would Paul or Larry, even though they despised Crockwell. Especially Larry."

"Is Larry an old friend of yours?"

"Not old, but good. We met in a bar in Albany when Paul and Larry were having some hard times on account of Paul's drinking. We slept together once in a while, especially after Larry moved out and had his own apartment. We turned on together occasionally, and one time we ran into Paul when he was drunk and he joined us. And that's when it happened. One Thursday night in January when they knew Crockwell would be alone in his office. They started talking about Crockwell, and they got angrier and angrier about what he does to gay people and what he did to them, and that's when Larry got this idea about how to get even."

He sat there breathing hard again, the wet circles under his arms as big as grapefruits now. He started to speak several times, but each time nothing came out. For a minute, I thought he might faint.

After another minute, I said, "Am I going to have to ask Crockwell what happened?"

151

Still breathing erratically, St. James nodded. "You can ask him. But I don't think he'll tell you."

"You realize, Steven, that there may be blackmail involved, and murder. You may be obstructing justice, a felony in itself."

Looking bewildered again, he said, "You keep saying that, but I don't understand it at all. Who would blackmail any of us? The only people who know about the incident are me, Larry and Dr. Crockwell. Paul wouldn't have blackmailed Larry, I can't imagine. And he didn't try to blackmail me. And even if he had tried to blackmail Crockwell, Crockwell would have just said, 'Okay, tell the world. Then you'll go to prison for what you did.' So why would Paul do that?"

"Maybe," I said, "Crockwell's reputation was at stake, and that meant more than anything to him, and so Paul knew he was vulnerable."

"That's possible," St. James said. "But Crockwell could have just said to Paul, 'Tell anybody you want. I'll just deny the whole thing. You're just a disgruntled former patient who went over the edge, and you're a drunken sexual pervert nobody will believe.' And anyway, Strachey, where did you get the idea that there are pictures? Nobody was taking pictures, I can tell you that for sure. I know, because I was there."

St. James seemed to be breathing more evenly and sweating a little less now, though his dogs were slobbering up a storm. I felt like getting down on the floor and slobbering too. It seemed as though I had systematically eliminated all useful knowledge pertaining to Paul Haig's death and that I was nearly all the way back to my state of useless innocence of five days earlier.

I said, "Steven, unless you can find it within yourself to be more forthcoming with me on exactly what happened in Crockwell's office that night, I do believe that I'll have no choice but to go to the Albany police and relay to them the admissions you have made to me here tonight."

St. James's fist came down on the end table next to him, causing the lamp on it to jump and the dogs to leap into the air and come down snarling. I left soon after.

152

21

Late Sunday night, back on Crow Street, barely un-
bitten by dogs and still bordering on the desperate, I considered
how the precious little I had left to go on was Vernon Crockwell
himself. Vengeance had been done to him—"tortured" was one
word St. James had used—and it was so awful (so humiliating?)
that Crockwell didn't dare report the incident, even though it was
a crime, an imprisonable offense.

So Haig had tried to blackmail Crockwell? And Crockwell,
whose reputation was everything to him, killed Haig? And tried to
kill Bierly? And did that mean St. James was next? I'd forgotten to
warn him. Though all that seemed less and less likely now anyway. Approached with a blackmail attempt, Crockwell probably
would simply have told Haig to buzz off. And Bierly, of course,
had been telling me all along that I was off base and on the wrong
track connecting the St. James–Haig–Bierly–Crockwell incident
to Haig's death, or even to any blackmail attempt at all. Yet Bierly
did try to implicate Crockwell himself in Haig's death. That's what
he had tried to hire me to prove.

Timmy was asleep when I climbed into bed, and I wanted to
chew it all over with him. But he needed his rest on account of
working for a living, unlike me, so I lay for some hours going
over it in my mind and awaiting a blinding insight. But by three
A.M., the last time I checked the clock, the only thing I had produced was some drool on the pillow.

Monday morning, first thing, I called Crockwell's machine—I had
nowhere else to turn until after I met with Paul Haig's Ballston

Spa psychiatrist that evening—and left this message: "Hi, Vernon, Don Strachey here. I know about your evening with Bierly and Haig and Steven St. James in January. You have my sympathy, but we do need to talk. You talk to me, or I talk to Al Finnerty. Take your choice. Call me."

Timmy, just out of the shower, said, "You were a little bit abrupt with Group Commander Crockwell. What was that about?"

I described my evening with Steven St. James and its tantalizing, incomplete revelations.

Timmy said, "I wonder what they did to him. Do you think they could have raped him or something? That's what it sounds like."

"St. James says no, they'd never do a vicious thing like that. Anyway, rapists tend to have histories of being violent, and none of these guys do, that I know of."

"I'll bet it had something to do with their being gay, though, and the psychotherapy group. Let the punishment fit the crime."

"Whatever it is, Crockwell is apparently so determined to keep it from coming out that he'll risk being charged with Bierly's shooting, or even Paul Haig's murder."

"You're not still planning on ruining Crockwell, are you? Even if he wasn't mixed up in Haig's death or Bierly's shooting? It does sound as if he may have suffered enough."

"Suffered, yes, but he's still operating his rotten, destructive business. Anyway, no. I'm beginning to suspect that there may be ways other than ruination to remove Vernon T. Crockwell as a social menace."

"Just to be on the safe side, maybe you'd better run those ideas by me first."

He ambled by me, naked, en route to his outfit-of-the-day, nicely laid out the night before across his personal ironing board.

"Maybe I will run my ideas by you, or maybe I'll just run them up your leg. Like this."

He hated being late for work, but once in a while he made an exception. He hopped off the bed half an hour later, reshowered, and sped off to the office of Assemblyman Myron R. Lipshutz

154

(D–New York City), for whom Timmy was chief legislative aide. And I drifted off and slept till one. It was lucky I woke up then, for I had slept through a call from Vernon Crockwell. His message on my machine said he could see me at three in his office, and I called his machine immediately to confirm the appointment.

"I hope you're not going to mention this perfectly idiotic blackmail business to the police, Donald. It will just fuel their misguided suspicions that I was involved in Larry Bierly's shooting or even Paul Haig's death. My attorney has managed to convince the district attorney that the evidence against me is entirely circumstantial and it's obvious that someone who doesn't care for me or my principles is attempting to frame me. But the blackmail idea will only get the police stirred up again, and that would be to the advantage of no one except the vicious deviant who is behind all of this."

"But Vernon," I said, "what we've finally come up with is a powerful and entirely plausible motive for Paul Haig's murder. Blackmail makes sense. And Paul's mother says he admitted to her—rubbed her nose in it, actually—that that's what he was attempting just before he died: the blackmail of somebody with enough money to pull Paul back from the brink of bankruptcy."

Crockwell sniffed. He was seated across his desk from me before his framed certificates in normalcy studies and his library of sexual normaliana. Both his hands were up within sight, a sign maybe that I had earned a degree of trust.

He said, "But I was *not* the person Paul was blackmailing. I repeat, I was *not* the person Paul was blackmailing. Once again: I was *not* the person Paul was blackmailing. Can you grasp what I am saying, Donald?"

"Yes, Vernon, but the question remains, Were you the person Paul was blackmailing?"

He wasn't used to this, it was obvious. One hand went back down behind his desk, and I doubted he was reaching for his checkbook. He said, "Donald, you obviously have nothing to

155

offer me in this matter, or to the cause of truth. I agreed to see you today only because you claim to have some information about me that you seem to think I may consider embarrassing. I suppose you think you're blackmailing me. Perhaps that's it—perhaps *you* are involved in some type of odious blackmail scheme."

"That's a whole new slant, Vernon. Maybe it's me I should be sniffing around. You're a genius."

"Well, you'll not blackmail me."

"What was it like?" I said gravely, and watched him.

He reddened and looked away. After a moment, he said, "Well, what do you think it was like, Donald?"

"They did it right here in your own office?"

"Of course. The equipment is here."

And I thought, Oh, the equipment, yes, the equipment. I said, "It was a Thursday night, right, Vernon? So Paul and Larry both knew you would be here alone."

"Yes." He was unable to look at me.

Now the question was, Who or what had they tried to turn him on to? I said, "Did they bring their own—what? Photos? Slides?"

He glanced at me quickly and seemed to relax a degree or two, as if I had missed something critical and especially humiliating. He said, "Steven St. James provided the slides."

Of course. Mellors. I remembered a visit Timmy and I had made to the Hudson Valley Game Farm several years earlier with Timmy's sister and her children. Recollections of the petting zoo came flooding back.

I said, "What were the the pictures of? Sheep?"

Crockwell shuddered violently once, then gave me a despairing little nod.

"They tied you up? Gagged you?"

"Yes," he squeaked.

"They wired you into your own setup—where is it, down the hall, behind those closed doors?"

"Yes."

"They wired you into your own Frankenstein's lab setup for zapping the bejesus out of men when they respond sexually to

156

other men, and they—what? Zapped you when slides of *Playboy* bunnies came on and then they shut off the juice when slides of sheep came on?"

Now he looked up at me desperately. *"Female* sheep," he bleated.

"Well, sure. They knew you weren't a pervert."

"No. No, the whole thing could have been worse." At this, he quickly looked away, and I began to wonder.

I said, "It was a brutal thing for them to have done to you, Vernon. Whatever foul deeds you may have committed against gay men in that room over the years, none of it was as vicious as what was done to you by Bierly, Haig, and St. James on that night last January."

"No, no. You can't even begin to understand what it was like, Donald."

"But were you . . . ? You know."

"Was I what?"

"Weren't you turned on, Vernon, just a little?"

"Of course not!" he snapped.

"My God, Vernon," I said, "do you mean to tell me that your system doesn't work? That in fact you can't change a man's sexual orientation with dirty pictures and electrodes and lightning storms? Wait till this gets out."

"Don't be absurd. Sexual reparative therapy using aversion techniques requires dozens of hours over a long period of time to achieve lasting results. Moreover, having intercourse with a sheep is not a natural human desire."

"I've heard from friends who grew up on farms that it can be quite pleasant, though."

Being a town boy, I guessed, Crockwell just glared.

I said, "Why didn't you call the police? After they left, I mean. How long did this go on, anyway?"

"From 10:40 P.M. until 1:45 A.M. It was endless, *endless."*

"I'm sure it was, Vernon. You must have been both mortified and terrified. What was done to you was a felonious criminal assault. So, why didn't you have the three of them prosecuted?"

157

He glowered and even shook a little. "Can you imagine the—the television coverage of such a trial?"

"Yes, I can."

"I would have been a laughingstock. My patients would have—lost confidence in me."

"It's like the old joke," I said. "A man running for sheriff in Texas wants to spread the rumor that his opponent fucks pigs. A campaign worker says, 'Why do that? It's not true.' 'No, it isn't,' the candidate says, 'but let's make him deny it.' Just being mentioned in a conversation about bestiality is bad for business, and being mentioned in this regard every night at six and eleven between the killer-mom stories and the Lotto drawing would pretty much end a man's professional usefulness in Albany, I would guess. I can understand your reticence, Vernon—although I'm not sure I would have been so forbearing in the matter myself. In fact, I'd have been left with feelings that were downright murderous."

He said, "Of course you would. I had such feelings too. I'm only human."

"But you didn't act on those feelings, Vernon?"

"No, Donald," he said. "I am not a murderer." He looked me in the eye when he said it, and he looked to me as if he either was telling the truth or was a total psychopath.

"You say Haig never tried to blackmail you. What would you have done, Vernon, if he had? What if Paul had come to you and said, 'Pay me sixty thousand dollars or I'll spread pictures around of you involved in what will look to a lot of people like some kind of ritual involving sadomasochistic bestiality'?"

"I'd have told him to take his sordid business elsewhere. First, there are no pictures. No one had a camera that night. Second, if Paul had spread the story of the incident, I would simply have denied it."

"That would have damaged your campaign for sheriff, Vernon."

"I wasn't running for sheriff, Donald. I'm a respected psycho-

158

therapist and Paul Haig was an alcoholic and a sexual deviant. In any case, I can't imagine Paul Haig attempting to blackmail me by threatening to make public an incident in which his—not mine but *his*—involvement was criminal."

I kept being reminded of that. I said, "You've got a point, Vernon. But Paul Haig was blackmailing someone, and then he was killed. The probability is high that the relationship between the two events is cause-and-effect."

"This may be true, but I think you need to look into Paul's life of depravity for your answers, not my life of professional integrity and Christian probity."

What a pill. I said, "How come for a while you were desperate to hire me, Vernon, to get you off the hook with the cops, and then you changed your mind?"

He blushed again. "I was acting irrationally for a period of time. I was too emotional." He blushed some more.

I said, "You were trying to buy me off. You knew Bierly was trying to sic me on you, and you knew I detested the savage things you were doing to men in your crackpot practice. So you thought that for money I could be turned into your ally instead of your adversary. But then you saw that my aim was to dig out the truth at any cost on Paul's death and Larry's shooting, and I wasn't going to care what I dredged up in the process—your going into training for sheep fucking and whatnot—and you decided you had better take your chances with mere legal representation and Norris Jackacky's chummy relations with the DA, and I could take a hike. Am I right?"

"Donald," he said mildly, "you could not be more wrong. My overture to you was sincere. I believed my best hope was to have Larry's assailant identified and charged—and Paul's, if there was one. And I believed, based on what Norris had told me, that you were the best man to do the job. The Albany Police Department is not as effective in these matters as it might be. It was as simple as that."

"Then why did you change your mind?"

159

"Well—on the advice of my attorney. He decided that your involvement was—redundant." He was blushing again, of all things.

I said, "I don't believe you, Vernon. Your suddenly distancing yourself from me had something to do with your night of woolly eroticism."

He shook his head. "No."

"Yes."

"No."

"What is it? There's more to the sheep story."

"No, there is *not* more to the sheep story."

"Anyway, how did they get up here that Thursday night? Doesn't the building have security?"

"There's no guard. I buzzed them in. Paul phoned me and feigned a mental breakdown. I was skeptical but let my compassion for a former patient whom I thought of as a lost sheep—lost soul—interfere with my better judgment. And I buzzed the door open from my office without knowing precisely who was going to arrive. It was a very great mistake that I will never, ever make again."

"Not exactly, I suppose. I think there's still a part of this you're not telling me, Vernon. Something you badly did not want me to uncover, and that's why you left a message for me on Saturday telling me to piss off."

"Absolutely not," he said, bright as a tomato on Timmy's Aunt Moira's kitchen windowsill in August.

I watched him radiate red heat and light for a quarter of a minute. Then the thing that should have been obvious all along hit me, and I said, "If Paul Haig was not blackmailing you or either of the two others involved in the allegedly unphotographed episode of *amour de brebis,* then he was blackmailing someone else about whom he had information that that person would consider damaging or even incriminating. Prime candidates surely are members of the therapy group. Paul presumably knew many of their most intimate secrets. Is that correct?"

"I suppose that would be true. Most members of the group,

160

however, tended to speak in generalities about their past unfortunate lives as sexual degenerates. So it would be hard for a blackmailer to come up with tangible or even specific evidence that could be exchanged for money."

"Were all the group members that discreet and closemouthed, or just some of them?"

"Two members of that particular group," Crockwell said, looking queasy, "were particularly graphic and loquacious on the subject of their own sexual perversions."

"Who were they?"

"You know I can't tell you that. But you can take my word for it, Donald, that for a variety of reasons neither man is a likely target in a blackmail scheme."

Moody and Stover. I said, "But some members of the group no doubt are likelier targets. And the incriminating dope Haig might have had on one of them could have come from a source other than a therapy session itself. Maybe a member wasn't succeeding in his de-queering nearly as well as he let on here, and he badly did not want that bad news to get back to—wherever. Whether or not any of that happened can be learned only by digging around extensively in the group members' lives, a project I might or might not have the time and resources to take on. I might have to leave it to the cops.

"The job can be narrowed down considerably, Vernon, if I know who in the therapy group might reasonably be expected to have the wherewithal to come up with sixty thousand dollars on short notice. If anyone knows who in that group has access to big bucks, it's you. You know who had a hard time raising the cash for treatment and who wrote a check without giving it a second thought. Are you going to help me out, or aren't you?"

He looked thoughtful, but it didn't last. "I can't tell you that, and I'm sure you can understand why, Donald. Patient confidentiality is paramount in my profession. The ethics involved here are clear."

"Yes, I know all about your ethics, Vernon. Look, I'm not asking about anybody's manatee fixation or whatever, only about their cash reserves, which is surely a fairly innocuous matter in the therapeutic context."

"Well, you are quite wrong about that."

"Oh. I beg your pardon. So you're not going to help me identify the person who killed Paul Haig and may have tried to kill Larry Bierly, two of your former patients?"

"No, I'm afraid that if it involves medically confidential information, I'm unable at this point in time to help you, Donald."

"Then you get no mercy from me," I said, and got up and went out.

22

My partially sleepless night and early-morning romp with T. Callahan had left me jet-lagged by late afternoon—sleeping until one hadn't helped—so I'd been pouring down extra-strength Jamaican Blue Mountain for over an hour when Timmy arrived home just after six. I didn't know then that my extra coffee consumption would turn out to be the key to an early resolution to the question of Paul Haig's murder. I just meant for it to get me through the evening without dozing off and toppling face-foreward in a public place.

I told Timmy about my meeting with Crockwell and the news of the therapist's onetime course in aversion therapy. Timmy stared at me in horror.

"Why, that's savage!"

"It is."

"You're making it up."

"No."

"But it's beastly!"

"Well, yes."

"But how could they do such a thing? Even to a man like Crockwell?"

"Two of them were enraged at him, they were under the influence of powerful drugs that break down inhibitions, and I guess they saw it as a kind of poetic justice."

"Oh, it's poetic, all right."

"Yes. Not Emily Dickinson, though. Robinson Jeffers maybe. Or Edgar Guest."

"It's poetic, but is it justice? I certainly don't think so. Crockwell's patients all went to him voluntarily, misguided as they were. But what those three did to Crockwell is assault, pure and simple. And he's not pressing charges?"

"No." I told Timmy the story of the Texan running for sheriff who wanted to accuse his opponent of fucking pigs.

Pouring himself a cup of the potent coffee, Timmy said, "That's a good joke about Texas politics, but it also illustrates why people who are victims of sex crimes often won't come forward and testify against the people who assaulted them."

"That's true, Timothy. But you also have to admit that (a) the joke is funny, and (b) it's a bit droll, too, when a man who cons people into administering electric jolts to themselves to combat their sexual natures gets a dose of his own medicine. Admit it. The image is priceless."

He poured one-percent low-fat milk into his coffee and stirred it. "But it's still assault."

"But the image is still priceless."

"But it's still assault."

"But the image is still priceless."

He conceded nothing. Though after a moment he did say, "Are there pictures?"

"No. Anyway, Crockwell maintains he never got it up for the sheep pictures. Or even for the *Playboy* bunny slides, would be my guess, given the circumstances."

"Well, there's that."

"Yes, think of the Polaroids showing up in the supermarket tabs. The horror."

Timmy shuddered, but I could see the images flipping along inside his head, and I suspected that they were not without entertainment value. He said, "So now you don't think Haig's blackmail scheme had anything to do with Crockwell and the sheep?"

"I'm pretty sure it didn't."

"But it's such a classic setup for blackmail."

"Not if there are no pictures or other evidence—which St. James and Crockwell both insist there couldn't have been—and

164

the blackmail target is ready to tell the blackmailer to go jump in the lake."

"I'm sorry, Don. I guess you're back to square one then."

"Not at all." I explained that with the Haig–Bierly–St. James (You-Don't-Want-to-Know)–Crockwell sheep incident now eliminated as the nexus of the blackmail situation, it was suddenly clear that the most likely blackmail target for Paul Haig would have been a member of the Crockwell psychotherapy group who was secretly involved in sexual escapades that would have been considered impermissible by both Crockwell and others in the man's life, and who moreover was in a position to come up with the sixty thousand dollars Haig needed to hang onto Beautiful Thingies. I said Crockwell wouldn't tell me who in the group was well-heeled and that I would have to find out independently. Meanwhile, I'd keep my appointment at eight that evening in Ballston Spa with Dr. Glen Snyder, who treated Paul Haig during the six weeks prior to Haig's death, and who I believed might have information or insights about Haig that would shed light on the blackmail or at least the circumstances surrounding it.

Timmy said, "If Snyder is a well-off shrink, maybe Haig was blackmailing him and he killed Haig. He would have known about the Elavil because he prescribed it."

I poured myself another cup of coffee and thought that over. "But what could Haig have had on Snyder?"

"I don't know. Pill pushing? Fishing out of season? Maybe Snyder put the moves on Haig, and Haig went along with it and got pictures secretly taken of whatever went on between them. It could be anything."

"I don't know, Timothy. That's pretty wild. But not totally off-the-wall, and while I'm talking to Snyder I'll keep your scenario in mind. And if I'm not home by midnight, maybe you'd better phone the Ballston Spa cops and have them take a look into Snyder's office. That's where I'm meeting him."

He said, "At midnight I'll be sound asleep. Do you want me to set the alarm and check to see if you're in bed?"

165

"No, I have a feeling I'll be home in plenty of time to tuck you in. Or to get tucked. Though I've drunk so much coffee I may be circling the house at six thousand feet for most of the night."

He said, "I'll dream of you up there."

I said I'd try to beam friendly messages down to him.

By seven-thirty the Northway commuter traffic had thinned out and I cruised unimpeded up through the spring evening. To the commuters in Clifton Park and the other northern suburbs of Albany, I-87 was something of a daily drag. But to Timmy and me, all of its associations were happy: It was the way to summer concerts at Saratoga, camping in the Adirondacks, weekends in Montreal for jazz and *blanquette de lapin*. I'd have been relaxed and eager driving north that evening if I hadn't been going to see a man about a murder, and if I hadn't drunk too much coffee and needed very badly all of a sudden to urinate.

I knew there was a Northway rest area above Clifton Park, and when I came to it I pulled in. The I-87 rest areas, in keeping with the intentionally woodsy, nature-friendly character of the highway, had no restaurants or gas stations, just restrooms, lawns, picnic tables and parking.

There were plenty of cars angled along the sidewalk leading to the restroom building, and I soon became aware of why some of them were there. My gaydar was rusty, but not so out of whack that I didn't instantly appreciate that this was a busy gay cruising area. After I peed, a number of pairs of eyes followed me outside, and I noted that men were coming and going behind the restroom building. A hole had been ripped in the wire fence at the rear of the rest-area clearing, and a path led away into the woods. In fact, this rest area had been notorious in fast-lane gay Albany for years, I remembered. And that's when it all came together.

23

The meeting with Dr. Glen Snyder was underly helpful but not a washout. He had no knowledge of any blackmail
attempt by Paul Haig, he said, but he did know from his own
sources that Paul's father had once been accused of trying to
blackmail a state official and had barely escaped prosecution.
Snyder knew too of Paul's desperation over his financial situation
and his fear that he might lose his business. In fact, Snyder had
prescribed the Elavil to alleviate what he called the "severe anxiety" brought about by Haig's financial crisis and the fact that his
personal life was pretty much of a mess.

Snyder said the last time he'd seen Haig, Haig had seemed less
stressed out. But Haig had made no mention of his money wor-
ries being over, and Snyder just thought the Elavil had begun to
do its work. Snyder said he was saddened and surprised to learn
in March that Haig had killed himself, and Snyder wondered at
the time if either Haig hadn't gone off his medication for a reason
unknown to Snyder, or some new crisis hadn't come along that
sent Haig tumbling over the edge into hopelessness. The likelihood of murder came as news to Snyder.

I asked him whether Haig had ever discussed the other members of the Crockwell psychotherapy group. He said only in a
general way. Haig talked about Larry Bierly, Snyder said, and
how wretched Haig had been over losing Bierly, and how he
attributed this loss to his alcoholism, which he feared he might
never control. Snyder didn't say anything about a Haig family
history of untreated alcoholism and I didn't bring it up. Snyder

167

said Haig's bitterness over being subjected to Vernon Crockwell's homosexuality-cure regimen was deep, but Haig's bitterness over, and inability to accept, his own unconventional sexuality ran deep too, and Snyder considered Haig a deeply damaged man.

No doubt he had been, though he needn't have died young. Paul Haig had survived AIDS, and gay bashers in high and low places, and Vernon Crockwell, and to some extent even his family. But in a moment of terrible weakness—and probably self-destructive revenge against his mother—Haig had reverted to a despicable practice his father apparently had originated in the family. The second time around, the act's consequences were even more dire than they had been the first time. Trying to blackmail a man hadn't just left an ugly cloud over Paul Haig's life; it had ended it.

Tuesday morning I called my credit-checker friend and said I would pay top dollar if she let me jump the queue in her work day and receive, at the soonest, all the financial dope she could come up with on these people: LeVon Monroe, Walter Tidlow, Eugene Cebulka, Roland Stover, Dean Moody and Grey Oliveira. I said I was most interested in Oliveira. I was told to call back in the early afternoon.

At ten A.M., I walked into Larry Bierly's room and said, "I know about the assault on Crockwell. Phyllis Haig was right when she told me you were a violent man. Paul must have told his mother some half-truths—a family custom among the Haigs whenever they weren't telling bald-faced lies to each other. It sounds like Paul made a habit of bad-mouthing you around Phyllis because that's what she liked to hear. But when he told her you had assaulted a man, he omitted the fact that he was there at the time and he was involved himself. And of course he left out the part about the electroshocks and the pictures of the *Playboy* bunnies and the sheep."

Bierly's little red numbers started going crazy, but he didn't call for the nurse. He looked at me big-eyed and said, "Did you tell the police?"

"No."

"Are you going to?"

"I doubt it. That's up to Crockwell, and he seems disinclined to have word of the episode bruited about the Capital District broadcast-ad market at six and eleven."

"We should never have done it. It was wrong. I know that."

"No, Larry, you should never have done it. Why did you?"

He tugged at the IV tubing leading into his arm and shifted his muscular bulk. "Drugs," he said.

"Right, the devil made you do it."

"I'm really *not* a violent person," Bierly said, almost plaintively. "It was some kind of bad acid or something that Steven and I got hold of. And of course Paul was drunk. He hardly knew what was going on, I have to admit. I was the one who made it all happen."

"You could serve time for it."

"I know, I know, I know."

"And that's why you tried to dump me from the case, isn't it? You suspected Crockwell had killed Paul and tried to kill you in revenge for the late-night aversion-therapy incident, but you couldn't even fill me in on Crockwell's only genuinely plausible motive, because it would have implicated you in a felonious assault. Then when I stumbled on St. James and started getting close to that unpleasant part of the truth, you wanted me out of the picture—even if it meant Crockwell would get off scot-free."

He nodded and looked away morosely.

I said, "Larry, if you thought Crockwell had killed Paul and shot you, weren't you afraid that Crockwell would go after St. James too? You didn't even warn him."

"But Crockwell didn't know who Steven was."

"Surely he knew Steven's first name from the night he met him," I said. "And I knew a man named Steven St. James was involved, and you knew I knew it, and you knew I was talking to Crockwell."

Bierly sulked guiltily. "Who told you about the—incident? Did Steven tell you?"

"No, he refused. I extracted it from Crockwell."

"Oh. So now are you going to be able to nail Crockwell?" Bierly asked, brightening a little.

"He didn't do it," I said. "Crockwell didn't kill Paul, and he didn't shoot you."

"How do you know?" He looked badly disappointed.

"Because I believe I know who did do it. I want you to think about something, Larry. After Paul died, did you mention to anyone that you thought he had been murdered and that Vernon Crockwell had done it?"

He chewed this over. "A couple of people, I guess."

"Who?"

"Dody, my assistant manager."

"Uh-huh."

"Ed Chartrand, who I have running Beautiful Thingies."

"Right."

"Probably a few others."

"What about my involvement? Did you tell anybody that I was looking into Crockwell's possible involvement? Or that the police were?"

"Just Dody. I talk to her about a lot of things."

I said, "What about a member of the Crockwell therapy group you were in? Are you in touch with any of them that you might have mentioned any of this to? Or did you run into one of them?"

"Just Grey Oliveira."

"Uh-huh."

"Grey came into Whisk 'n' Apron one night recently—it was some time soon after I had dinner with you last week, I think—and I got to fuming about Crockwell. I told him a lot of people didn't think Paul had really committed suicide, and both you and the cops were investigating Crockwell. I might have exaggerated the situation a little. Do you think Grey had something to do with Paul's death?"

"Yes, I think Grey murdered Paul. And if he had killed Paul and had learned that the cops and I were investigating Paul's death and we suspected Crockwell, he could have buttressed those suspicions of Crockwell, first by sending the cops the therapy-session tape that shows a nasty conflict between Crockwell and you and Paul, and second by shooting you on a Thursday night, when he knew Crockwell would have no alibi, and then by planting the gun in Crockwell's dumpster."

"Jesus!"

"You played into his hands with your hatred of Crockwell, which blinded you—and me."

"But, God, what would Paul have had on Grey to blackmail him with?"

"I plan to question Oliveira about just that. An excellent possibility is, he's the member of the therapy group who Paul caught in what he described to you as a wild scene in a tearoom. Paul never told you who that was, right?"

"No."

"Did he say where it was?"

"No."

"But it happened during the period Paul was traveling once a week up the Northway to his psychiatrist in Ballston Spa, if my chronology is accurate."

"That sounds right, yeah."

"That's the route Grey takes home to Saratoga every day after work. Did Oliveira have much money that you know of, Larry?"

"I have no idea," Bierly said. "I don't think he ever talked about money in the group. Grey was always just kind of polite and reasonable. He was rather sarcastic sometimes, and I got the idea once in a while he was putting us all on—especially Crockwell—and that he was just going through the motions of staying in the therapy program because for some reason he had to."

"I've spoken to Grey," I said, "and he admitted to me that that was the case. He went to and stayed with Crockwell because his wife asked him to, he told me, even though he had no hope for, or interest in, succeeding at being zapped straight. He struck me as being an extremely cynical man. In fact, I think he worked hard at portraying himself to me as a cynical and amoral man of a certain not-too-unusual type in order to keep me from suspecting him of being a hard and cynical man of another, rare type—

a man who kills people in cold blood in order to keep what he wants to have."

Bierly said, "That's absolutely horrible if it's true. Can you keep Grey from getting away with it?"

"I think so," I said. "But first I want you to get out your checkbook. Then I want you to call up Vernon Crockwell and apologize for trying to turn him on to farm animals, and tell him to get out his checkbook too. Then I want you to ring Phyllis Haig, taking care to catch her before noon, and tell her I said I want her to apologize to you for calling you a murderer and a buttfucker, and she had better get out her checkbook too."

Bierly stared at me open-mouthed for a long moment, and then he said, "If you say so."

At one-thirty my credit-check agent confirmed what I had suspected: that none of the former members of the Haig-Bierly-Crockwell psychotherapy group had any net worth to speak of, and that while Grey Oliveira's assets were proving harder to pin down, his cash flow was ample enough to suggest net worth well beyond what one might expect from a state employee who commutes to work every day.

I phoned a friend who grew up in Saratoga and still runs his family's restaurant there and asked if he knew Grey Oliveira. He said sure, Grey was a town fixture. Grey was not originally from Saratoga but had married into an old town family. Annette Dreher, Grey's wife, was a horsey-set Saratoga hostess and benefactress and an heiress of some means.

When I phoned him at his office at the State Division of Housing and Community Renewal, Oliveira flirted with me in his dry, crude way and agreed to meet me for a drink at six at the Broadway bar where we'd met the week before.

Then I dropped by Al Finnerty's office to fill him in and to ask to borrow some police equipment.

24

So, it's Albany's numero-uno private dick. Land any big ones since I last saw you, Strachey?"

"Nah. How about yourself, Grey?"

"Me? I'm not the dick, that's you. Though from where you're standing you could probably spit and have it land on a few people who think I'm kind of a prick."

"I'll bet."

He gazed at me with those eyes. "Get you a beer?"

"I could force one down."

He signaled the bartender and I asked for a Molson. Oliveira shifted on his stool as I eased onto the one next to him. He seemed to sense that something was different, but he wasn't going to act as if he was in a hurry to find out what it was.

I let him pay for my beer, and then said, "Are you still sucking every dick you can stuff in your mouth up and down the Hudson Valley, Grey?"

He froze for about half a frame before going on. "That's not a very good come-on line, Strachey. I'm not particularly romantic, as you might recall. But if I had made the first move, I would have come up with something a hell of a lot sexier than that."

"I didn't mean it as a sexual icebreaker, Grey."

"Does this mean that you're going to break my heart, Strachey?"

"You told me on Friday that you've made it a rule to have sex only with two people, your wife and your married fuck buddy, Stu. You described this situation as an AIDS-safe closed circle.

But I have the impression you make exceptions to your rule."

"On rare occasions, yes. If I believe a man to be both well-endowed and healthy, I have been known to follow my glands down whatever happy trail they may lead me."

"If you believe him to be healthy. That sounds unscientific, Grey."

He shrugged. "It might not pass muster at Oak Ridge, but of course this is Albany."

I said, "Does your boyfriend Stu also participate in high-risk unsafe-sex orgies at the Northway tearoom between Albany and Saratoga? Does your wife?"

Now he looked grim. "Have you seen me there? I've never seen you. And I'd remember you, Strachey."

"I've only stopped there once."

"And you saw me and I didn't see you? I hope I wasn't back in the woods bent over with my drawers down around my ankles."

"I didn't see you there," I said. "Paul Haig did."

He blinked, maybe because his heart jumped. "He did?"

"Yes."

"How do you know? What makes you think that?"

As the bartender passed us, Oliveira threw him a quick glance. Oliveira was aware now of all the people around us and that we were holding what he knew would be an exchange that could change his life, and it was happening in one of the most public of public places, a white-collar bar during happy hour. I wasn't crazy about the milieu either—it lacked dignity.

I said, "There are photos of you, Grey. Did you think that you got the only copies, that there weren't others?"

He blinked again, three times, and then studied my face. He said, "I'm not even recognizable in those pictures. They're dim and out of focus. Those pictures are shit."

"Then why am I here?"

He swigged from his beer. "Fucked if I know."

"Let me lay it out," I said. "Please correct me if I'm wrong in any of the details." He watched my lips form words. "Paul Haig desperately needed money," I said, "to save his business. After he

174

caught you in some wild scene in the Northway tearoom, he checked up on you to see how much you were worth. When he discovered that you had access to your wife's big bucks, Paul came back to the tearoom during the evening orgy hour, caught you again, and—presumably with a hidden camera—repeatedly took your picture committing lewd acts." I waited.

"There were five of us that night," Oliveira finally said conversationally. "Paul joined in part of the time. It was a hot scene and he was as big of an animal as anybody else there. The rest of the time, when he wasn't participating, he was acting as a lookout, he said. I remembered later he had a Beautiful Thingies box he was carrying, and the camera must have been mounted in that box somehow."

"That sounds plausible, Grey. Then Paul must have contacted you soon after the event—at work would be my guess—and he informed you that if you didn't cough up sixty thousand dollars, he would see to it that your wife received copies of the photos."

Wincing, Oliveira said, "He actually mailed copies of the pictures to me at my office at HCR. If my secretary hadn't been out sick on the day the envelope arrived—she probably had the rag on—she'd've opened the envelope herself probably. Luckily, I got to it first. After that, Paul called me and said it was another set of photos and the negatives that I was supposedly buying from him."

"Right. That's how a thoughtful blackmailer would handle it. So you made an appointment then to hand over the cash in return for the negatives and extra prints?"

"At Paul's apartment on Willet Street," Oliveira said casually, as if he were describing the site of a pleasant small dinner party. "Paul wanted me to deliver the money on a Wednesday night. But I said it would take me until Thursday to round up that much cash."

"Grey, I'm impressed. You were planning that far ahead—already setting Crockwell up as a suspect in case anybody saw through the 'suicide' scenario. You're quite the planner."

"That's the area of my training and expertise," he said,

nodding. "I'm not just a planner, I'm a professional planner, and a damned good one too." When I just stared at him, he added, "I know what you're thinking, Strachey. You're thinking, If only this bright young man with his darkly brooding good looks and his hypnotic gray eyes had applied his talents in the cause of good instead of evil, what a boon that would have been to him and to mankind. Isn't that what you're thinking?"

"Something like that."

"Well, 'Of all sad words of tongue or pen, the saddest are these: It might have been.' John Greenleaf Whittier. It's the one thing I can remember from junior high. Don, are you ready for another Molson?"

"I'm fine."

Oliveira caught the bartender's eye and signaled for another draft.

I said, "How did you get Paul Haig drunk that night, Grey?"

"Easy," he said. "I brought a bottle and opened it. I suggested we toast the successful completion of our business transaction. Paul thought that was a wonderful idea. He was extremely nervous, and I suppose he figured a good stiff drink would calm him down. And it sure did. And his second drink, and third, et cetera, made him even more loosey-goosey."

"And then you—what? Discovered the Elavil in the bathroom?"

"On the bathroom sink when I went in to take a whiz. The container was nearly full, and I thought, 'Well, my my, such a stroke of fortune. Now I won't have to shoot him.'"

Oliveira's beer arrived. He dug a couple of bills out of his pants pocket and laid them on the bar.

I said, "That was lucky, not having to make a loud bang on Willet Street, and a bloody mess in Paul's apartment."

"I bought the gun off a kid on the street in Brooklyn one time. So it could never have been traced back to me. But still, if Paul had, quote-unquote, 'shot himself,' the police might have wondered where he got the gun, and so forth. So the Elavil was definitely better. Paul was blotto by the time I found the pills, so

I helped myself to about fifteen. They were high-milligram, high-powered little fuckers, so I didn't have to feed him the whole bottle and risk him puking everything up all over the both of us. I mashed the pills up in the kitchen and stirred them into his next drink, and then I stayed around until he finished the bottle. While he was drifting off, I tapped out the goodbye-cruel-world suicide note on Paul's computer. By that time, I could have used a second drink myself. My own share of the fifth came to about a teaspoonful, and that was damn fine liquor that Paul got to drink. Paul went out with style, as only a Haig should. There's no need for Phyllis Haig ever to know about any of this. But if she did have to know, she'd find some solace in the fact that in providing the libations that eased Paul into his eternal rest, I did not stint. It was the finest Glenlivet."

I wanted to rip him to shreds, but instead I swigged from the beer bottle. I said, "So that was the gun you shot Bierly with? And then you tossed it in Crockwell's dumpster?"

"Yo, you got it."

"What if Bierly had died from the shooting? What had he done to deserve that?"

"Not a thing, really. But I ran into Larry at the mall, and he told me that you and the cops suspected Paul's death hadn't been a suicide. So it made sense to further fuel everybody's suspicion of Crockwell—I'd already sent the tape to the cops, understand—by popping Larry and trying to pin it on Crockwell. But I didn't shoot to kill, and I really am glad ol' Lar pulled through. He could use a sedative himself once in a while, but overall Larry's okay in my book, and I wish him all the best."

I said, "The tape you sent to the cops along with the anonymous note pointing to Crockwell in Paul's death—where did you get it?"

"I'm not sure. Radio Shack? Kmart? Now you're straining my powers of recall."

"My question is, Who recorded the therapy session? You?"

"Naturally. Who else would?"

"But how did you know to record that particular session? Did Larry tip you off that he and Paul were quitting the program that day?"

"And that I'd need the tape of that angry scene six months later to throw suspicion on Crockwell in Paul's death? Hey, what am I, the Psychic Friends Network? I taped that session, Don, my man, because I taped them all."

"Why did you do that?"

Now he looked at me with his big, lovely eyes much glassier than when I'd arrived, and with an odd little smile. He said, "I taped all the sessions because I figured that sooner or later Annette—that's my wife—would catch onto the fact that I'm totally, insanely, expialidociously man-crazy, and I'm getting fucked by half the men in eastern New York and western New England. Then she'd throw me out on my ass without a dime. And to maintain the lifestyle to which I have become accustomed, I thought I might blackmail other men—men in the therapy group, guys in the tearooms, you name it. I don't know whether I would actually have done it—or really thought I could ever get away with it—but I did fantasize about blackmail. The tapes were my security blanket. And then that wussie drunk Paul Haig showed up and he tried to blackmail me. Ironic, isn't it? I love it."

I sat and looked at him. Who was Oliveira? How did he get this way? He had told me at our first meeting that he had had an alcoholic, abusive father. But so do lots of people, and they are not psychopaths. I said, "Well, it's all over now, Grey. You're through. You're done. You'll be locked away for—in effect, the rest of your life. You can't get away with what you did to Paul Haig and to Larry Bierly."

"Yes, I can," he said.

"Nope. You can't."

"What's the evidence? Those blurry pictures? That's circumstantial. There's no way to connect them to Paul's death or me to Paul's death. If anybody asks me, I'll deny everything I told you. If the cops start bothering me, my wife's father will hire the best

178

criminal lawyer in New York State, and if all the prosecutor has to go on is some cheesy blackmailer's smear pictures and the word of some nancy private dick from Albany, I'll be sent back home with an apology. And then the Drehers will sue your queer-boy's ass for every nickel you own, which I would guess from the looks of those cheap scuffed shoes and that raggedy-ass jacket you've got on is about ten cents."

I took another swig of beer. Then I said, "Where'd you get the taping equipment to record the therapy sessions, Grey? Did you steal it from the taxpayers of the State of New York? Was it from your office?"

"Jeez, Strachey. Do you think you can get me on petty larceny? Do you think I'm a damn thief? Really, my friend. I bought all my own equipment."

"Well, that clears that up, Grey. You're right, you won't be charged with stealing taping equipment in addition to your other crimes. By the way, are you recording our conversation today? Are you wired right now?"

"No, Strachey, as a matter of fact I'm not wired."

I said, "I am."

He looked at me, then at the bottles lined up on the shelf straight ahead of him. After a minute, he looked back at me. His hands were shaking. He said, "Too bad a beautiful hunk like you had to turn out to be such a flaming asshole, Strachey."

I shrugged.

He said, "Prison life. Yuck."

"It's undeniably a step down from Saratoga."

"How's the medical care in New York state prisons?"

"Variable, I suppose. Not the best, Grey."

"Jesus. I've got these lumps in my armpits and groin. I hope it's not what I think."

"You were fucking all those people and you've never even been tested?"

He only managed to shake his head twice before I got him by

the collar and dragged him off his stool and out the door to the waiting police cruiser, where I was threatened with arrest for assault if I didn't release Oliveira immediately, which I did after hoisting him to a height of about five feet.

25

Timmy said, "You seem to have been shortchanged by Phyllis Haig."

He had his calculator and her check made out to me in front of him on the kitchen table, and he had concluded that the daily rate she had paid me came to about forty dollars.

"Although," he said, "since you're triple-billing people on this case, you'll still come out ahead."

It was Friday evening and we were celebrating the end of Timmy's work week with Indian take-out and Danish beer.

"I'm not actually that far ahead," I said. "I'm cashing Phyllis's check and billing her for the unpaid balance of many hundreds of dollars. And I'm cashing Bierly's check too—but not Crockwell's. I'm returning his check. I don't want his money."

"Sure you do."

"Nope."

"Why? It's ill-gotten, but better you than he should get to spend it. Better it should go toward our mortgage than Crockwell's."

"He'll need every dollar he's got," I said. "Crockwell is closing his practice and he's going back to school for retraining in a different field. I spoke to him this afternoon."

Timmy said, "I'm flabbergasted," and he looked it. Then, suspicion setting in, he said, "Why did he happen to confide in you regarding this major career change?"

"Cuz we're buddies."

"No you're not. What have you done?"

"This morning," I said, "Dody, Larry's assistant manager at

181

Whisk 'n' Apron and Beautiful Thingies, called me and said she'd found an envelope stuffed in the back of a file at Beautiful Thingies. She opened it and it contained odd photographs."

"Uh-oh."

"Larry told her to show them to me, so I drove out and took a look. Some were copies of pictures of Oliveira on the loose in the Northway rest area. They were pretty murky, but collectively they did seem to be Oliveira, so my pretending to him that I had copies of the pictures, even when I didn't, wasn't quite as cheap a stunt as it seemed at the time."

"Not that it mattered," Timmy said in an uncharacteristic burst of moral relativism. "What were the other photos of?"

"Bierly, St. James and Crockwell all insisted to me that no one had photographed the aversion-therapy assault on Crockwell. But someone *had* taken pictures of the gross event, because that's what I found in the envelope. And when I asked him today, Bierly remembered that Paul did have a Beautiful Thingies box with him that night, and he could have had a camera concealed in it. Apparently he did, for I am now in possession of an envelope stuffed with inexpertly photographed but still decipherable images of Vernon Crockwell in alarming sexual proximity to the back end of a small—though presumably not underaged—ewe."

Timmy's jaw dropped, but not for long. "They brought an *actual live sheep* in there? Don, the poor sheep!"

"When I confronted him the other day, Bierly chose not to mention that particular aspect of the incident. And it's the one thing Crockwell couldn't bring himself to tell me until today. They didn't actually try to force the sheep on him—or him on it. It was just there for atmospherics—aroma therapy and so forth."

"No."

"Yes."

"And you went to Crockwell with the pictures of all this and you—"

I nodded.

"No. No, you can't."

"I did."

"You blackmailed him into shutting down his program? Forever?"

"I negotiated a settlement in lieu of cash for my services rendered in getting him clean off the hook in Paul Haig's murder and Larry Bierly's shooting."

"But—that's appalling!"

"No it's not. You're appalled, but it's not appalling. Think of the hundreds of gay men I'm saving from Crockwell's torture chambers and his lunacy. I should get the Nobel Prize for mental health."

"But people go to Crockwell voluntarily, Don. It's education, education—education about the nature of sexuality and about homophobia—that will save people, not—not some sleazy type of blackmail."

"Both have their places," I said, "with people as dangerous and unsalvageable as Crockwell. Timothy, I fear we're never going to agree on these things."

He said, "No, Don. We're not." Then he sat quietly for a few minutes while he finished off the fish vindaloo.

Breaking his sulky silence, Timmy finally said, "So what's Crockwell's new profession? Or didn't you have the nerve to hang around and ask?"

"Oh, Vernon and I had a real nice visit," I said. "He grew up in Chicago, but he said he'd always had a hankering to head out west to the wide open spaces. His wife's from Wyoming originally, and she's talked for a long time about resettling there. So Vernon sees this move as an opportunity. He said he thought he might try his hand at ranching."

Timmy looked at me carefully. "You're making this up."

"I am not."

"Okay then. What kind of ranching?" He was starting to brighten up again.

"Llama," I said, and I could tell he didn't know whether to believe me or not.